The 1975 Apocalypse

Jonny Halfhead

For Dan Moult, thank you.

FOREWORD

Although it may seem hard to believe, the only fiction in this short story is the plot. The opinions, views, experiences, attitudes and beliefs are all very real and have been experienced the world over by millions of Jehovah's Witnesses including myself. I have seen and heard first-hand the expressions and beliefs portrayed here.

As such, this story is dedicated to the millions of unsung heroes that have suffered at the hands of this terrible cult and found the bravery to leave it, even though that means losing an entire world, including all family, friends, colleagues and tribe. I am always humbled and in awe at the strength that every ex Jehovah's Witness has and I salute all those that lost that battle and felt so alone that they took their own lives. The abuse and suicide rate in such a small community is so high that it is pandemic. I hope and pray that the world and those still trapped in the religion continue to wake up to the monster that is in our midst.

There is a growing support network. If you need help or just need to know that you are not alone, please visit xjwfriends.com

EVIDENCE 569832A
STEVEN MCPHEARSON'S DIARY

27TH AUGUST 1974

This is my first entry in what I know will be an unprecedented period of time in human history. My peer, an Elder in the congregation, suggested from a wonderful talk at last week's meeting, that because of the time we are living in, it is our holy duty to record the events about to happen around the world. He advised the congregation to put pen to paper and create a diary, so that we can all look back in a thousand years and never forget the wicked world in which we once lived. We will have been lifted out of the old world and witness what God did to save his righteous people.

I immediately saw the benefits and couldn't wait to get started. I've also instructed my wife to start her own diary as well. We have been married for just a few weeks now and she is the most wonderful person I have ever met and I cannot wait to spend eternity with her. Her name is Anna and she is 18 years old. She is strong willed, very spiritual and full of confidence and has made a wonderful wife. I am 24 years old and a man of responsibility in the congregation and hope to soon be a circuit overseer myself by the time I am 30 years old.

For those who will read this centuries from now, I know I will need to explain where I am in time and why I am so excited and poised for the great changes about to come very soon. At this moment in time, the whole world is ungodly, except for a couple of million true Christians that organise themselves under the name of "Jehovah's Witnesses". As an organisation, we are waiting for the time when God will rid the earth of the unfaithful and ungodly and leave just the few to live in a perfect paradise on Earth forever and to live a life of servitude to God on a paradise Earth. The war will be called Armageddon and I will be amongst those numbers that survive it.

We know that the change from this world to the next is imminent because we are blessed with the full understanding of the Bible and the Bible shows us that the end time is right now.

I have a mixed feeling of both fear and excitement. The end of this world is going to be violent and horrific to witness, but the people of this world have had their opportunity to change their wicked ways and join us to salvation. I really struggle to understand why they refuse to see what we see and save themselves and their families. If I had children, I would do anything to make sure they were safe, not only in the here and now but also in the future.

But children are a luxury for after Armageddon. This world is no fit place for children of any age when the prospect of a better world lies so closely. So, I have decided that we will not have children this side of Armageddon and wait for the New World to have them.

It is so very exciting. Of all the ages of man that I could have lived, I get to live in the time period when one world ends and God's New World arrives. I will be here when billions of wicked will be destroyed and I will be amongst the privileged faithful to go through to a new paradise world. What an awesome time to be alive.

EVIDENCE 569832B
ANNA MCPHEARSON'S DIARY

24TH SEPTEMBER 1974

This is a most exciting time. I wanted to chronicle my life at this very important part in human history. I start this diary in September 1974 and hope is high that The Society have their figures worked out correctly and that Armageddon is right on our doorstep. I want to write this diary for the thousands of generations from now that will no doubt wonder what this legendary time would have been like from a personal viewpoint.

My name is Anna. I am 18 years old and have been married now with my new husband Steve for a month. We call our organisation Jehovah's Witnesses. We need to do this because the rest of the world needs to know about God; they need to know his name and have the opportunity to survive God's coming war called Armageddon. The world I live in is populated with nearly 4 billion people and yet there are only one and a half million Jehovah's Witnesses worldwide, so we need to make ourselves known and having a name for our organisation helps us do that. Using God's name, we will be blessed.

I sincerely intend to be honest and truthful about everything in this diary. Honesty and truthfulness not only make me a good Christian woman and wife but also help shape me as a better person. I look forward to being a good wife for Steve and devoting my love and support to him. Lately, there are too many women in the world not behaving like devoted wives and demanding equality with men. It sickens me to see women undermine their duty to their husbands. How is the world supposed to function if women try to demand equality? I have happily given up my part time job now that we are married so I can support my husband by being a dutiful wife. I fully intend to become a full time Pioneer and serve Jehovah God as well as my husband.

I love my husband Steve so much and I'm really looking forward to spending my life with him. I'm a strong person and I know my strength will help Steve to also be a strong and good person. We are the McPhearsons and as a unit we will be successful and loved… I just know it.

Pioneering is a promise to The Society to spend 90 hours per month preaching to the world about God, and to try and save as many lives as possible before Armageddon arrives. We go to everyone's house and knock on their doors and try to persuade them of the doom they are about to be swept up in and to show them that we can help them save themselves.

I have a mix of excitement and also fear of the coming of Armageddon. No one individual knows if they will be saved when God decides to rid the world of evil. I do not know for certain if I am pure enough to be survive, but I try with all my heart and soul to devote my life to God and my husband and to be a person full of virtue.

There is a growing sense that God will spring into action soon. God speaks to the Society directly through the Governing Body, a group we refer to as The Society. The Governing Body are a group of dedicated men that God speaks through to the rest of the Jehovah's Witnesses organisation and they have passed down to us the news that October 1975 is very likely going to be the date of the coming Armageddon. God will wipe out all those that do not believe in, and worship him and those that do believe will be spared and given eternal life on a paradise Earth. The prospect of Armageddon does frighten me a lot. I have grown up with the fear of a nuclear man-made Armageddon through the still raging Cold War between the USSR and America. The prospect of a nuclear war, nuclear winter and the horrors that would bring, would scare me even more if I didn't have such a strong faith in Jehovah and knowing that he would never allow that to happen to his Earth and his people. I feel so strongly for those that don't have that comfort that I have, that God will not allow nuclear war to happen because the Earth has been reserved already for the faithful.

I had a part time job for about a year until I got married. It seems a bizarre thing to try and explain what a job is to those who – in a thousand years' time – may have no concept of what I mean by it. We do not currently have the freedom to grow our own food and live off the land, nor have the opportunity to grow food for our congregation so that others have the time to do the much needed preaching work. In order to eat and to provide shelter from the weather, we have to conform to the current way that this world works. That means working for money. Money is a hard concept to explain, needless to say, that a few in this world have a lot and the many have little. In order to have the basics of life, the masses have to work for those few that have all the riches. Some in the congregation find ways of trying not to conform with this basic fact of life by working for themselves, but of course they still have to use money, which in turn is still working for the rich man's system.

Steve, my husband, works full time for one of those "rich men" in order to feed, clothe and put a roof over our heads. When he gets home, he devotes his evenings to godly matters and the pursuit of becoming more than a Ministerial Servant and rising to be an Elder. That is the hierarchy in the congregation and the expectation of every man to aspire to serve the congregation as one of the local Elders and I will support him totally to accomplish that.

The evenings are getting shorter, which means that summer is firmly behind us now. We have already had a couple of cold days and the larger coats have been pulled out from the cupboards ready for the oncoming autumn. I don't like the cold of winter. Doing the preaching work when your toes are numb from the cold can be very testing. Preaching is so very hard to do at times. I know that I am out there to save people's lives, but they really don't want to be saved it seems. Some are ignorant, rude and occasionally threaten violence. It is so hard to understand why they will not see what we see; why they won't open their eyes. Sometimes, I can get very down when I think of all those people that will die at Armageddon. But then they are being given a chance, an opportunity to turn their lives around and become one of Jehovah's Witnesses.

I think that Armageddon cannot come soon enough sometimes. This world just seems to get worse every year. Men on the television are dressing up in women's clothes, glitter and make-up. Homosexuality has become legal. There are strikes galore around the UK with power cuts, riots, free love and so much hatred. The Society tells us that the worse things become, the closer we are to the end and things really are getting terrible in the world. Thank goodness I have a husband, my family and Jehovah to look over me.

13TH NOVEMBER 1974

At last I have a bit of spare time to update my diary. It's always the same isn't it? You start off with the best of intentions to undertake a task - like this diary - and before you know it, a couple of months have passed and nothing has been added to it.

My hard work is paying off already. I undertake a few essential job roles in the congregation, which shows my enthusiasm and desire to get along and achieve a greater role. All is on course for my plan. Anna has started Pioneering which also shows a united front to everyone concerned and the Elders are responding to my enthusiasm. There are many that just don't seem to understand how simple it is to get on in the congregation. You just knuckle down, do as you're asked and get on with the jobs that need doing. I won't be spending too long doing the drudgery jobs around the Kingdom Hall.

The weather is starting to turn. It's getting colder and the nights are getting shorter. It's been raining a lot over the last couple of weeks which does make it harder when I need to be getting plenty of hours done in the preaching work. There is so little time. I spend most of my time working at a warehouse in the day to earn money. It's tiring and cold work.

I don't really like mixing with the outside world at all but, in order to feed my wife and I, I have to work. My warehouse job forces me to mix with people I would never choose to have anything to do with under any other circumstance. These people don't have any love for God at all. They are filthy in everything they do. Their language is disgusting, they talk about sex all the time in the most awful way and they behave exactly the same as they did when they were all at school. Nobody really grows up at all. I have to shield my wife from it all and leave that influence at the workplace.

Every day that I go home, I feel like I am dragging depravity along with me. I need to shower, not to just get rid of the days literal work filth, but to rid myself of the colourful atmosphere I spend eight hours a day under the stain of. I do spend quite a bit of work time trying to talk to my work colleagues about God, but they just laugh and poke fun at me. At least I get to count the time that I spend trying to preach to them towards my monthly reportable preaching hours. That is what matters more than anything else.

There was an incident at work just last week. There was a new starter at work and I saw an opportunity to try and talk to him about the Bible. His name was Paul and he was a young man, quite shy and quiet and looked lost and venerable against all the world-weary men around him.

Another shop floor worker took great offence at me talking to Paul about God. He went off on a tirade about me wasting work hours preaching, about not actually caring about Paul at all, just wanting to look good for "the God squad". There are a couple of other men from my congregation at my workplace and the floor worker asked me why I couldn't be like them. They only talk about God if someone asks them and even then only in break times, not during working hours. I think they show a bad example. God comes first before any worldly place of work. If there is an opportunity to preach it must be immediately seized upon, time shouldn't be wasted tip toeing around. I have God's work to do. The end is coming very soon and these people need the choice now. Fall in line or perish when God's wrath is unleashed on the Earth.

I was taken into the supervisor's office because the argument with the shop floor worker got very heated and in a small moment of frustration, I threatened to take him outside and teach him a physical lesson. It didn't get to that before we were ordered back to work.

My focus does not lie with work at all. Work is a means to an end. It puts food on the table and pays for the roof over my head. The most important daily task is serving God and not serving man. I need to preach to as many as I can in the short time the world has before God comes and destroys them. I don't really get mad with people; they get angry with me. I know if they don't listen to what I have to say, they really will live to regret it and very soon. I know I shouldn't, but one of my guilty pleasures when getting harassed by a worldly person about my faith or the way I conduct myself, is to let off a little titter when thinking about what will happen to them when God's wrath comes. They will be dead and I will be alive and reaping the benefits of a God loving way of life.

EVIDENCE 569832B
ANNA MCPHEARSON'S DIARY

28TH NOVEMBER 1974

I've had a bad day today. It's been so very cold. I really didn't want to go out and go from door to door preaching God's message, I just wanted to stay in bed. My feet are still like blocks of ice. I am very pleased with myself. My Pioneering is going well. Every month I've been getting my 90 reported hours in. I make sure I'm always home to cook for my husband, Steve. I'm not great at cooking, but I'm picking up tips from the other friends in the congregation. I love being with my friends; it always fills my heart with love and warmth when I can spend time with them.

The reason I'm in a bad mood apart from being cold to my core is an encounter out on the ministry - the preaching work - with a young woman who was so very horrible to me. Sometimes this happens. I'm out there in the freezing cold trying to save people's lives and some of them come back at you with so much anger. I struggle at times to understand the outside world. They just will not listen and don't care what we are trying to do for them. I'm trying to save their lives!

The lady in question was behind one of the doors I knocked on today. She was middle aged and as soon as she opened the door I knew from her facial expression that the conversation was about to get interesting. The lady had been reading a newspaper article about a young Jehovah's Witness who had died because he refused a blood transfusion and the young man's family had all agreed to let him die. The more detail the lady spoke about, the more her voice raised and the angrier she got. I tried to explain calmly that the Bible forbids any form of blood to enter the body. I even had the scripture opened out in my Bible to show her the passage, but she wasn't interested in listening at all.

She got so loud, shouting at me on her doorstep, that I knew I wouldn't be able to get through to her, so I left and walked away. This seemed to provoke her more as she swore abusively at the top of her voice as I retreated. My heart was pounding and my adrenaline pumping. I had to go and find a nice warm cafe to sit down and have a cup of tea.

Thankfully that doesn't happen too often. I just cannot understand why they get so angry, except perhaps because they know it's the truth we are giving them and they don't want to face it, so they lash out instead, perhaps? I want to love everyone I meet, so when I'm faced with nothing but contempt and anger, it's like a smack in the face. It leaves me reeling. I love people, my husband and my friends. How can it be so upsetting to folk when all I want to do is share some of this love and also save their lives?

Steve has been feeling down lately. He says the men at work know he is a Jehovah's Witness and make fun of him for it. Sometimes it gets on top of him and he struggles to argue about the Bible with them. He's been told to not mention it at work - which we disagree on - because I think he should use every opportunity to try and save his work colleagues lives. I have noticed that he has started having a drink every night - just a couple of beers - but I worry he may be relying on it as a means to unwind at the end of the day. God warns us how easy it is to get ensnared in vices.

I enjoy being married, but it's not everything I expected. In fact, sometimes quite the opposite. I love Steve so much, but after the first couple of weeks of being married, things between us changed slightly. It's hard to put into words exactly what I mean, but there's a dynamic between us that had gone so quickly after we were married. The passion between us has subsided sharply. All that waiting to have sex with the man I love and, eventually, it was a little disappointing on the wedding night. The whole marriage experience hasn't been what I imagined it all to be.

Steve doesn't like me spending too much time with my friends and family. I love my friends dearly, but with all the work I'm doing and being a good wife to Steve and having everything prepared for him, I'm struggling so much to find time to make sure I can see my friends. Some of them have already told me how Steve makes them uncomfortable when they visit our house. I don't want my friends to be uncomfortable when they come to see me. I'm not mad with Steve at all, but there must be some way of reaching a compromise.

I'm determined to stay strong. There are always ways

around every problem. I'm sure that I can find a balance; a happy medium for everyone.

EVIDENCE 569832A
STEVEN MCPHEARSON'S DIARY

2ND JANUARY 1975

I've always struggled with playing politics. There seems to be nothing more annoying that trying your best to succeed and watching other people that do very little get promoted and favoured above you. This has happened this week. I know I'm supposed to be humbled and loving and warm to my fellow brothers in the congregation, but the way things work internally seem more and more worldly than I would have ever imagined.

There are growing cliques that form in the congregation. Groups of Elders and Ministerial Servants - the wannabe Elders - silently battle and tug against each other for political space. I expected some small amount of ego clashes but nothing to the extent that I am seeing. I work patiently and constantly remind everyone that I am here, eager and waiting in the wings ready for another, bigger assignment. But things seem to have gone cold and others around me appear to be getting more favour even though they say they do a lot, but actually they do very little.

I suppose it could be argued that I am acting jealously and I suppose I am. I also wonder if this is a strong lesson, to fight a little dirtier, to be more realistic if I want to make the grade in this arena. Maybe it is time that I got my elbows out a little and made more of what I do instead of silently expecting my works and actions to be noticed.

Yes, I have decided that this is war. It's time for me to roll my sleeves up and properly play the game. There is no room for diplomacy anymore. I must pick my sides and make my intentions very clear and very loud and - of course - towards the right people.

Anna thinks I should just stick to what I have been doing. She says that God will reward me if I am patient. But I know that God will not want a servant to be so quiet and humble that he cannot help himself. If I cannot go and get what I want, how will I have earned it and how can I protect the congregation as a man of direction and decision if I cannot do those things for myself? I know God will reward those that fight to please him.

I have observed that there is a clear self-appointed "leader" within the Elders of the congregation. A man that clearly thinks of himself, and acts, superior. I will closely side with him. I'll take him out for a drink - I think - and invite his family round to our house for dinner. Of course, flattery always works as well. I could copy a few of his mannerisms and styles. He does like to do extra-long prayers at the beginning and end of a meeting. He also always goes over the allotted time at studies and meetings. I think I could learn a lot from copying that man and if I make it blatant enough, he should notice that I'm honouring him as well.

I know he likes his football. I think a bit of swotting up on his team and getting together with him to have a few drinks and watch a match will also be a great way to get close to him.

This diary is great. It allows me to think out loud and it gets my grey matter going. It also helps when I read it back as a sense check. These plans are amazing; I'll be an elder in no time. My fellow brothers had better watch out!

EVIDENCE 569832B
ANNA MCPHEARSON'S DIARY

13TH FEBRUARY 1975

I don't generally get much time for this diary. God keeps me very busy. I had to write today though because otherwise I would just scream from shame, frustration and anger.

I really don't get much spare time at all. Each day I am up and out of bed early to prepare my husband's packed lunch for work. Once he leaves the house I then need to get cleaned up, made up and dressed up to go out on the ministry and knock on people's doors and preach. By mid-afternoon I'm back home and doing some more housework, ironing, washing clothes before getting my husband's dinner ready for him for when he comes home from work. Then three times a week it's off to the Kingdom Hall for the services, or on one of the other four days of the week, self-Bible study or study preparation for the other Kingdom Hall services. It never stops. I hardly ever get any spare time at all. I don't know how other couples find the spare time to have children.

Steve and I have decided not to have children yet, and wait. Armageddon is coming very soon and it will be wiser to have our children in the New World rather than right here and now. The Society does encourage couples to wait as well, so we follow good advice.

I have no spare time and Steve has so little spare time as well. If I spend more time on the ministry, other duties get neglected. It's such a difficult balancing act. For a couple of weeks, I've let things slip a little. I've picked up quite a few Bible studies with people I have been preaching to and seem responsive while going from door to door. Bible studies are the next stage after someone shows an interest from a regular door visit. It's the beginning of a fruitful relationship as you train them in the doctrines of the Jehovah's Witnesses beliefs and then teach them about the best chance they have to survive the oncoming war between man and God.

I have a few Bible studies every week now. That has pushed my other duties aside somewhat. I haven't been able to do as much housework and a couple of times I've been late with dinner for Steve when he gets home. Steve is my husband and I am his wife and as his wife it is my role to make sure he is fully supported so that he can become one of God's ministers, an Elder in the congregation. Getting behind in my chores means that I have been neglecting him and not properly giving him the full support that he needs. I am also struggling in my wifely duties in the marital bed also. Steve is not a very romantic lover at all and I find myself struggling to take an interest when he makes his sexual advances. I know my duty. I never say no to him, but he complains that I don't show any enthusiasm either. I try and fake interest as much as I can, but I'm growing so tired of late that it gets more and more difficult to show interest. I do find it a little disturbing that he doesn't seem to love me enough to even know when I'm putting on a show and not being myself when it comes to our intimacy. He really doesn't seem to care at all except to get his regular dose of sex.

I know I have neglected my husband, but nobody warned me what might happen; what the consequences of my neglect might be. The Society hasn't warned me and neither have the other Sisters or my friends in the congregation. Today I found out when everything came to a head.

It's Thursday night. Thursdays are always very tight on the day's schedule. The Kingdom Hall services start at 7pm; we have to be getting ready from 6pm. Steve doesn't get home from work until after 5:30pm, so I have to have his dinner ready on the table as he steps in the house from work. I had a bible study today which overran by quite a bit so I spent the rest of the day playing catch-up. Then to make matters worse, the dinner I was making took longer than I had anticipated to cook. When Steve came in at exactly 5:30pm, half the dinner was still being cooked.

Steve had a stressful day at work today and I could tell as soon as he came through the door that his day had been a tough one and I didn't ease that stress at all.

The situation blew up so quickly, I just wasn't expecting it. I was on a back foot as soon as he arrived and he started to shout at me because I didn't have his dinner on the table for him. I knew I shouldn't have, but I shouted back at him. I suppose I felt so very guilty for allowing for such an oversight. Steve relies on me to be prepared for him. Answering him back just made the situation worse. We were both screaming and shouting at each other for nearly half an hour, at which point the dinner was completely ruined anyway.

Once we realised the evening was ruined, the argument subsided a little and Steve grabbed a couple of cans of beer and went upstairs to get ready for the Kingdom Hall. That left me to clean up the ruined dinner and sob my heart out for 20 minutes.

I was so far behind by that point I knew I would have to make my own way to the Kingdom Hall anyway. Steve would have to take the car; he had duties to perform at the Kingdom Hall and he couldn't tolerate being a minute late. I still hadn't even got cleaned up and changed when we met in the hallway. With Steve on his way out and I on my way upstairs to get myself cleaned up, the arguments and shouting started all over again.

It had only been less than a half hour but Steve's mood had stepped up a gear with an even greater urgency, annoyance and frustration. I just wanted to get ready as I knew the walk was going to take me a long time. I didn't want to pick the argument back up again, but we met in one of the doorways. I was going into the bedroom to get changed and Steve was on his way out while frustratingly straightening his tie. Steve stood in the doorway and blocked me from passing him. Without warning all hell broke out and we were face to face shouting at the top of our voices at each other. I could smell the beer on his breath and I saw the anger and intense hatred in his eyes. Adrenaline ran through my body like acid and made me shake all over. I just wanted to run - I think I should have done - as I suddenly felt a huge thump in my abdomen. Steve had struck out with his fist straight into my stomach. I felt a shockwave in slow motion shudder through my torso and out to my arms and legs and the wind left my body in a sudden rush. I fell to the floor hardly able to breathe and doubled over in tremendous pain.

How things got that bad so quickly, I just don't know. It was unbelievable how fast the situation had escalated and then just as quickly, everything went quiet. Steve had turned and gone out the door so fast that my knees had hardly reached the floor before he was gone.

Then there was a total silence.

It seemed like an eternity before I could get my breath. I was on my knees bent double on the floor, trying to get any air into my lungs while feeling my stomach striking out loudly with acute, agonising pain. Eventually the air came in a huge intake, followed by a rush of uncontrollable tears.

My entire world went dark. I wondered how the situation had escalated so badly? I did everything that was expected of me. Surely what matters is that I try to do everything as best I can? I thought Steve and I loved each other. Why would he do such a thing?

My head was spinning with so many questions. Even though my thoughts and heart were sinking quickly into a very dark and lonely place, I knew I had to act quickly. That self-indulgent, lonely place is where the devil resides; that low place where I am vulnerable is the chance Satan will take to fill my head with doubts and questions about my marriage and persuade me to move away from my faith.

I picked myself up off the floor, my stomach in such horrendous pain, knowing this was likely Jehovah's test. This was where I really had to prove my faith, where it counted and very much mattered.

I felt so sick. I could feel the muscles in my stomach throbbing. I made my way to the bedroom to try and finish getting ready to go to the Kingdom Hall. I knew how important it was to make sure I went to every meeting at the Kingdom Hall. I knew that one day there would be a call, an announcement, something that would trigger that the end of this world was coming and I didn't want to be one of those that would miss out.

When I tried to change my dress, the pain in my stomach just doubled me over onto the bed. I wailed in agony, despair and frustration. I just wanted to get on with a normal life. Once again, stray random thoughts started to spark across my brain. I thought about Steve who was already likely at the Kingdom Hall and I wondered what he was doing. Was he in a sorrowful state of tears and regret, taking a moment to have a sorrowful, remorseful confession in a quiet side room? Or was he just putting on a smiling face and shaking people's hands like nothing had happened? I strongly suspected the latter, but argued with myself that the Devil was putting those thoughts in my mind and I tried to get my mind back on track. But my body was having none of it. Every time I moved, my stomach ripped with pain, until instead of getting dressed I spent the next half hour vomiting in the toilet.

I eventually gave up going to the Kingdom Hall and just fought with myself, my mind and my body in bed, alone all night. My thoughts went without my body to the Kingdom

Hall. My mind and heart met up with my friends and chatted and laughed even though my body ached and screamed with pain. All my friends and everyone at the Hall was sympathetic and wanted to help and gave me oceans of sympathy. It was beautiful, loving and warm and nearly dulled some of the pain, until it hit again and again all night long. My body, my head and my heart screamed out loud. I could feel my friends drifting away as they felt alienated by Steve and they knew that some things - no matter how close you are to your friends - are just personal matters within a family. I wanted to telephone one of my friends and tell them what Steve had done to me, but I knew the trouble I would involve them in if I told anyone about this.

So I suffered alone.

Steve never came home that night.

EVIDENCE 569832A
STEVEN MCPHEARSON'S DIARY

20TH FEBRUARY 1975

In some ways, Armageddon can't come quickly enough. The idiot worldly men at work treat me with such distain; I can't wait to see their faces when they realise how wrong they have been to reject my preaching to them. At least things are going well at the Kingdom Hall. I'm becoming quite close friends with an Elder who has now also become a Mentor. His name is Ben. We meet a few times a week and either study and prepare for the meetings or have a few drinks and watch the football. He can really put the booze away, which surprised me a lot.

There's always hierarchy in the congregation. Many think they are so spiritual and goody-goody that they make me sick. I'm sickened by some of things I see. I think Armageddon will clear out a few from in the congregation as well as outside of it.

Anna has been worrying me lately. She doesn't seem to grasp how difficult it is to keep up appearances and to keep my position moving up in the congregation. I had a word with Ben and he advised me that we are in a very difficult time before the end of this world. Women are developing thoughts of independence and power, more than any other time in history and we as men have a duty to make sure that free spirit is kept in check. We need to love our partners, but we also need to make sure we keep our house in order.

Anna has been late with her timekeeping and worse than that, not had dinner ready when I get home. It has happened a few times now and last week it blew up and became something harrowing. I had to physically put her in her place. It was not pleasant at all. I'm already losing all respect for Anna only after a really short period of marriage. Marriage has not been what I expected it to be.

There's a small part of me that feels some guilt that I have had to get physical with Anna, but she knows that the only way we can both become strong in the congregation is if we have the respect of our peers around us. It will all be worth it when I become an Elder and then who knows where we can go from there.

I do have to think of the possibility that Anna is not the one to be with me for the long term. I met a wonderful, bright and powerful worldly woman a couple of weeks ago. I know I shouldn't be thinking about it, but this woman turned me upside down to the point that I cannot stop thinking about her. My mind has been rushing at a million miles an hour wondering if I could convert her to the faith and maybe there is a chance that somehow God will bless me and my circumstances could change. I know it hasn't even been a year that I've been married to Anna, but I'm not even sure if I love my wife anymore. Anna really doesn't seem to share my dreams and desires. Anna really wants to have children, and children are the last thing I need at the moment. That would scupper my plans to expand my influence in the congregation and further. Children aren't frowned upon, but it is generally thought that so near to Armageddon is not a wise time to be having children. Despite the common sense of it, Anna still keeps bringing the subject up. I just don't have time for children right now. I also know that we really cannot afford to raise children either. Work out there is scarce at the moment; the whole country seems on the verge of civil uproar. No-one knows if they will have a job tomorrow, so having children is a very unwise choice.

The name of the woman I met is Julie. For some reason we can just talk forever about even the most trivial of things. I have never had that connection with Anna before. Julie is warm and receptive. Every time I meet her, I do feel very guilty though. I can see how this may look from an outside point of view. I know how I feel about it. I am losing affection and sympathy for Anna and warming more and more to Julie. Every day I ache to see Julie and try and find ways to make that happen. I have no plans with regards to Julie; I haven't set out to have an affair and I cannot just walk out and leave Anna. I have worked too hard in the congregation to allow it all to be thrown away for a quick act of selfish passion. But still, it doesn't stop my mind constantly wondering about Julie and wondering what Julie wants from me. Every time I think of Julie, it excites me - which also surprises me and catches me unawares.

My mind is a whirlpool at the moment. I need to get

control of my life and get everything back on track. Armageddon is coming and I need to be correctly positioned and prepared for it.

EVIDENCE 569832B
ANNA MCPHEARSON'S DIARY

2ND MARCH 1975

It's been a couple of weeks since the big argument between Steve and myself. I've had to stay at home and away from the meetings as I have been hardly able to eat much and I still feel so sick. My stomach has been bruised really badly. I was very conscious of making sure nobody knew what happened between Steve and I. I realised that I stepped over the mark. I have become argumentative and haven't been supporting my husband as well as I should be doing. It's no wonder he lost his temper. I love my husband so much. I know that if I just give him an overabundance of love, he will love me back with the same intensity. Love will always win out every time.

Steve has been different since that day. He hasn't told me that he was sorry, but I can tell. We have been quite close this last couple of weeks and nearly like we used to be when we just got married last year.

Because I have had to stay at home, I have been lonely

for a couple of weeks. No-one has been to visit to check if I'm ok. I can only assume that Steve has come up with some convincing reasons why I haven't been around for a while. I feel so alone and isolated. I hate to think what my life would be like if I didn't have Steve around. I'm so proud of him. He works so hard to be a good Christian. He deserves to be an Elder and hopefully soon that will come.

The house seems so cold of late. Steve is working so hard that I don't get to see him much. He is either at work, out on the preaching work or studying with the Elders or doing his congregational duties. Sometimes he gets home at 5:30 for his dinner and then I don't see him until midnight most days. Sometimes I can smell the drink on him after he has been studying with the Elders, but I know that just helps the night's studying flow a little easier.

Sometimes I let myself think that Steve should perhaps show a little more remorse for hitting me. I know I'm to blame just as much and I have told him how sorry I am numerous times over the last couple of weeks, but Steve hasn't said anything back to me. His quiet demeanour tells me a lot, but it can never be as good as actual words. I am so disappointed in marriage. I know that I shouldn't say that and writing it down in this diary is a little dangerous. But then God sees all, so I can hardly escape judgement for anything I think and feel.

I know I need to keep quiet about what happens between the two of us. What happens between us is nobody else's business anyway and I don't wish to bring reproach to Steve or myself or our good standing in the congregation. I know in myself that although I may have deserved it in a way, I know Steve punching me was wrong.

But it is our matter to remedy and not anyone else's. Besides, God will guide us if we make sure we are doing his work and obeying his laws. I'm sure in my heart that Steve knows he shouldn't have punched me and I'm very sure that it will not happen again. I can see the guilt he feels in his eyes.

I'm determined that there will be no repeat of what happened a couple of weeks ago. I will work harder to be a better wife for my husband and work harder to support him as God wishes me to do. This is a new chapter in our lives.

EVIDENCE 569832A
STEVEN MCPHEARSON'S DIARY

18TH APRIL 1975

I'm in turmoil. I have had the most amazing news this week. I have finally been made an Elder. I'm well on the way – even at this relatively young age – and once I have consolidated my position as an Elder I will be looking to move further on from there. I'm so happy and at the same time so very torn.

Anna has made such a change and made so much more of an effort to support me over the last month that I can only feel great guilt. I had stopped seeing Julie, even though she is such an amazing person and totally different to everything else in my life at the moment. Although a part of me has wanted it, nothing romantically has happened at all between Julie and myself. I tried a couple of times to move our conversations towards God and to try and get a feel for how the land lies in regards to bringing her nearer to God. I don't think there is much of a chance that Julie will be convinced to become a Jehovah's Witness. She is just too independent and strong willed, which is why I am uncontrollably attracted to her. It is because of that I have made a concerted effort this last couple of weeks to steer clear of her. However, my resolve is already starting to fade quite quickly. I really miss Julie. I miss her smell, her laugh and her opinions. Everything about her is so refreshing.

I spend so much of my time thinking about Julie. Every time I do, I feel guilt towards Anna. Anna really has tried to be the perfect wife lately, but that just makes the waters murkier. I honestly don't think I love Anna anymore and seeing a once confident young woman lowering herself to please me just leaves me cold. I pity Anna and I can't help it. I'm starting to see Anna as someone quite pathetic who I have little respect for. Then in contrast - whenever I think of Julie - I see the total opposite.

I'm very aware of what I am writing here. The Society warns us all the time of the pitfalls of worldly women, how they are loose and have no moral guidance. I'm very aware of what I lose if I let my feelings be known to Julie. I have said nothing to her so far and I fight myself to supress any ideas or feelings that go through me when I am in her prescience. I'm not even sure she feels the same about me. She doesn't show any signs in the same way that I don't. If the situation progressed between us, I could lose absolutely everything I have worked so very hard for. And then of course, what about the impending war of Armageddon? In such a critical time, I really would be an idiot to lose my focus now, right here at the very end of things. Maybe that is it. Maybe this is my final big test from God before the end. If this is the end though, do I want to spend an eternity with Anna? I'm really not sure that I do.

Is a small moment in time with Julie worth a sacrifice of

eternity? The way I feel at the moment I don't even know. I'm even contemplating that it is. What is wrong with me? I don't doubt my right to be an Elder, my right to be in a position of power in the congregation or even to question that being an Elder is about power. Some of the Elders view their position as a slave to the congregation, as a service to the families and to the flock, but my eyes have always been open. Being an Elder is having power and I want more. Should I really be throwing that away for an undefined period of time with a woman I hardly know? My logical head says that I would be an idiot, and yet, every time I think about Julie, which is constantly, I get a warm rush of emotion and excitement, to the point I would be willing to throw everything away. The abandon of all logic in itself is refreshing and exciting.

What do I do? What am I thinking? It's a good job this diary is safe and hidden away. The choice would be taken away from me if anyone found out.

EVIDENCE 569832B
ANNA MCPHEARSON'S DIARY

2ND MAY 1975

I am so proud of Steve. He has been working so hard now that he has become an Elder in the congregation. I just wish we could spend a little more time together. I work hard to make sure his life as an Elder is fully supported. I turn my life upside down to give him the best opportunities in the congregation. Any success that Steve acquires is success for both of us as we are a team. Is it too much to ask that once in a while we get a chance to spend some time together?

I have asked God. I don't know if that is selfish or not. Steve is so busy. In a typical week, I only see him for one evening and even then he will likely be studying or on the telephone. A lot of the time I don't get to know why he is not at home or even where he is. He could be having an affair and I wouldn't know about it. That would worry me if I didn't know the amount of work he has to do.

I'm also concerned with how much he is drinking as well. Every night when he climbs into bed, I can smell alcohol on him. I have tried to talk to him about the problems he faces looking after the congregation but he tells me regularly that he deals with very sensitive and confidential matters in the congregation that he just cannot share with me at all. I do accept that, but it doesn't change the fact that at times I think we are drifting apart.

All of this is not helped by the fact that I notice a greater divide in the two distinct personalities that Steve seems to display. The public Steve, the one that shakes hands with everyone at the meetings along with the broad and friendly smile and warm words of encouragement, is becoming further from the version I see at home. Sometimes I see more of the public Steve than the private one, which is in a way a good thing as I'm not sure that I like the private Steve of late. He is becoming angry and aggressive once again. On the rare occasions when we are alone together at home, the air is tense, incendiary and filled with oppression. I fear many times as we swap short angry words occasionally that the violence may return. The anger in his eyes is frightening.

Twice last week, Steve didn't even come home and stayed out all night. When I quizzed him about it, he got very defensive and told me that some things are happening in the congregation that I'm best not knowing about. I do feel for him. The workload must be awful, so I try my best to carry on supporting him.

I've decided that I am going to make an effort to get closer to a couple in the congregation called Mary and Ben. Ben is also an Elder and is a close friend of Steve, something I didn't actually know until recently. It seems that Ben has been a sort of mentor for Steve over the past few months. I even found out from Mary that Steve goes around regularly to their house to have a drink and watch football. I didn't even know Steve liked football at all. How have I missed that part of Steve's life?

I have decided that it would help Steve and I get closer if I make an effort to get to know Mary and Ben better myself. I invited them to our house for dinner one evening last week which went very well. This way I may even get to see more of my husband. Plus, I could really do with a close friend and as a wife of an Elder. Mary would be a good person to have as a friend. I used to have a lot more friends before I got married. I have so little time for them now and I miss the company and I really need an understanding ear and a shoulder to cry on at times.

All the wives talk together when we are at the meetings and there is a general consensus that something is happening, not just in the congregation, but also in the world. As the year progresses, it seems there is a growing expectation, an air of change. It is whispered around with some excitement that perhaps Armageddon is so very close that within a few months, God's final war with man on Earth just might begin. We all agreed that there is a mix of nervousness and excitement. Will we finally be rid of the wickedness in the world, but also will we survive? Will God see good in our hearts and spare us? It is an amazing time to live, but an unnerving one as well. Does anyone actually know with any certainty that they will be chosen to live because of the goodness in their hearts? Steve is very sure that he will get through. He says that it is his duty to get through and organise the survivors to build a new perfect world for everyone to live in.

I just don't know. I try with all my heart to be a good wife and be a good person. I hope with all my heart it is enough. I love all the people around me. I go out and try to show love to the people in the world and try to save their lives. It is heart breaking to think that all those people out there in the world may die at Armageddon. I try not to think about it too much. The mothers, the children, the amount of death and destruction that is looming for the world. It's enough to send someone crazy. It's those times when I let my imagination wander that I start to feel that - just maybe - it is wrong to kill and destroy all those people in the world outside our Kingdom Hall. But it's those thoughts that we are told is the devil adding doubt in our minds. So I try and change my thought patterns. That's the problem when alone. Fighting those thoughts and those doubts gets harder. We are taught from the Bible, "the devil makes work for idle hands".

I love my husband, I love my friends and I love the congregation. We all have to work to maintain relationships. I will remain strong for myself, for Steve and everyone around me!

EVIDENCE 569832A
STEVEN MCPHEARSON'S DIARY

11TH MAY 1975

I am leading two lives. It's starting to bother me a lot. Out of those two lives, I know which life I want and it isn't the one I've been working towards for the past few years.

I had to put pen to paper again as Anna has made me so angry. I had to get away from her for a short while and vent my frustration into this diary. Anna knows how I feel about the subject of children, but once again she dropped hints about it. It makes my blood boil. She knows how I feel about it. Besides which, there is now another element and reason why children are not a good idea at all.

I had a chat to Ben, my Elder mentor and close friend over a drink, and he backed me up and told me with Armageddon being so very, very close, that I am right to stick to my decision. He is right. If I stay on this current path, bringing a child into this world is not very wise. Whereas if we wait just a short while, we have an eternity to have children. Anna and I have had this discussion so many times and I have told her very clearly that we are not to have any children and we are to wait.

I'm fighting myself with the choices before me. I've started seeing Julie again and spending time with her has tipped the balance away from my old life towards a new life with Julie. I know that it's stupid as I now have the responsibility of being an Elder. I have a wife and a life already made for me. Then of course there is the impending doom of Armageddon. If I'm on the side of sin when the end comes - and it is so very near - I will die along with the billions of other unrepentant sinners in this world. As if that wasn't enough, if I chose a life with Julie, that would mean my excommunication from the Jehovah's Witnesses. I would be disfellowshipped, punished, cast out and rejected by every single person I know in my life. They would all be told to turn their backs on me and to not even acknowledge me in the street. This would used as a shock, a hit of tough love to try and bring me back into the fold. Apart from Julie, I would be totally alone.

It's not much of a choice is it really? Everything including everlasting perfect life on a paradise Earth with my wife, my family and those around me in the worldwide congregation, pitted against Julie, isolation and death. Any sane man would tell me what an idiot I am. I would strongly council myself against it.

Yet, despite the logic, despite the clarity of common sense, despite the onset on world change and the threat of being shut out and an impending death, I know I have already chosen Julie.

I wanted to go on further from being an Elder. Age was

on my side. I was without children, clean and full of ambition. I wanted to become a missionary or a Circuit Overseer; the whole world of possibility was open for me. I have to say it though, I deeply love Julie. Now I also know that Julie loves me. Last week we slept together. It was so amazing that I didn't want to go home to Anna. I have fallen for Julie with all my heart, but I know that there are still choices I can make. I could still try and convert Julie and try and build my political life back up again with Julie by my side. But that would take years and Armageddon is more imminent than that.

If I am to rescue this, I would need to keep my mouth shut, stop seeing Julie and stick to the life I have and go with the logical, sensible and living decision. That was the choice I made just after leaving from sleeping with Julie last week. But, after a couple of days of deciding one way, as the week progressed and I dearly missed Julie and really missed the great sex, I went again last night and slept with her again. I seem to be unable to control myself with Julie. Being away from her is like withdrawing from a drug. I just cannot think of anything else and just want to go straight back to her again.

I'm determined to keep this my dark secret until I can figure out what I'm going to do. I am very aware that I'm burying my head in the sand, but at least for the time being, the great sex can continue.

EVIDENCE 569832B
ANNA MCPHEARSON'S DIARY

15TH MAY 1975

The house is very quiet. It's a good opportunity to update my diary again; my only true friend outside my relationship with God. It's been a horrible day. It's four in the morning and I cannot sleep. The pain in my ribs is unbearable. Every time I try and lie down flat, the pain in my ribs stabs me and jolts me, which in turn hurts my ribs, over and over. I'm scared, scarred and alone.

Steve didn't come home at the usual time for his dinner yesterday. It happens sometimes so I didn't think too much of it, but I was annoyed that half the dinner was ruined and that he hadn't called to tell me that he wasn't coming straight home. He didn't turn up until after 10pm and like other days before, he stunk of drink. I made a comment to him that I had missed him all evening and tried to tell him how lonely I was feeling of late. I then made a mistake of hinting how a child in our lives would give me focus and stop me feeling so alone.

That sparked off an argument that then moved into a massive tirade of anger from Steve which quickly turned violent. Steve first got hold of my neck and then punched me in the ribs so hard I was left winded again on the floor for quite some time. Steve just left me lying there, got his coat and left the house and disappeared.

I spent the next couple of hours hardly able to breathe. I couldn't stop sobbing and crying out with pain and heartache. I slumped into a well of despair and sadness so deep I didn't have a clue how I was going to climb out of it. I don't understand how you can do something like that to someone you love. That just made me question more if Steve actually loved me anymore and if he didn't, how scary that was. Could this go even further next time? I didn't want to think about that. I didn't want to be scared for my life with my own husband. Steve is under pressure - that's all.

My crying constantly jarred my ribs and made the pain even worse to the point that I eventually had to call an ambulance. I was taken to the local hospital, given an x-ray and told that I had two cracked ribs. Of course I lied about what had happened and how my ribs became cracked. That bothered me because a true Christian doesn't lie, but I was sure that it wasn't wise to bring shame on the congregation and on my family so I decided to not even give a hint of the truth while at the hospital.

The sun was coming up by the time I got back home the next morning and yet Steve still wasn't back home. I felt so isolated and alone and in great pain. The doubts and fears came back again and I had to constantly fight with myself and where my thinking and feelings took me. Steve eventually came back home later today and he was very apologetic, with promises that it would never happen again and that he would never again lay a finger on me in anger, just as he had last time this happened. It's difficult to not be sceptical.

I love my husband and I worry that he may not be showing as much Christian love as he should be. I worry that when Armageddon comes, he will be on the wrong side and won't be with me into the New World. I don't want my husband to die at Armageddon. I still love him dearly, but at the same time I can't keep going like this. I wonder where his regression will go. I wonder what will happen next time.

Steve and I had a really heartfelt talk and I realised how much pressure he is still under as an Elder and that the pressure just seems to be growing. I was very careful with my choice of words with him and although every part of my being wanted to confront him about his drinking, I knew that I couldn't solve this myself. I knew from our discussion that I needed a sanity check. I needed another viewpoint, someone to confide in and get advice from. Steve talked about Ben being his advisor and mentor, so immediately I thought about talking to Mary, Ben's wife.

Steve finished our discussion with his promises that he will sort himself out, that he just needed time, and begged me to not say anything about my broken ribs to anyone. I kept the marks on my neck hidden from Steve. I know that if he saw those it would spark something off again and I know they will be difficult to keep hidden from everyone, at least for a few days.

After we had our calm discussion, we both went to the Kingdom Hall for the meeting. There I met Mary and pulled her to one side to have a heartfelt chat and ask for her opinion. I was very careful about what to talk about and what not to disclose. I kept the conversation just to my worries about Steve's drinking and the fact that I had noticed it more and more. Mary confided in me that she was also worried about her own husband, Ben, and how often he drinks as well, although she never gave any hint that it was anything other than just concern and that his drinking had any other connected issues.

I tried not to make a scene and burst out in tears in view of everyone, but Mary could see that I was obviously concerned and upset. Mary advised me that I should pray for Steve as he is under considerable pressure, as all the Elders are at the moment at such a special time with the new kingdom being right on our doorstep.

I sit here now, unable to sleep and in great pain wondering what Mary meant. Does Ben talk to her more openly about what is happening in his world as an Elder? Steve tells me very little, if anything at all, about what he sees or hears or about what is planned or happening in the congregation. He's very closed and secretive like that. Are there signs already that the end is getting imminent? Have there been directions from The Society about being prepared? Is it really starting to happen?

I sit here alone, quiet and wondering how Mary can just tell me to pray for Steve. I've shown real concern and have confided in her about Steve's drinking and yet she doesn't offer to talk to Ben about it or have any wiser words than "leave it in God's hands". I know that is right and proper to a certain extent, but in many ways it just doesn't help at all. There was very little reassurance in that statement. Mary's reaction has left me cold and feeling rejected. I can't help but start to think of myself. If I give my life to support Steve, that seems to be getting me nowhere, except in hospital.

I can feel myself fighting my emotions internally, between my faith and self-preservation. I know I need to be patient and pray and leave it in God's hands to rectify. Maybe this is one final big test right at the very end to see if I am deserving of being in God's New World. Deserving to spend an eternity in paradise.

EVIDENCE 569832B
ANNA MCPHEARSON'S DIARY

6TH JUNE 1975

I had hoped that my broken ribs were a lesson so extreme that it would have shocked our relationship back on track and the air would be clear to start afresh, but that was a pipe dream it seems. I tried to keep the matter as quiet as I could. I didn't want to bring any reproach on Steve. The punch to my ribs left me in pain for more than two weeks. I wasn't able to go on the preaching work and couldn't go to the meetings either. I just told everyone that I felt unwell and just needed to rest up for a short while to recover. Steve had been telling me for two weeks how much he was sorry and that it wouldn't happen again. My ribs bruised in deep colours of orange, purple and black and I was very careful to keep the evidence hidden away. For a couple of weeks, Steve and I were the best of friends again.

The peace didn't last very long.

On Sunday, we had been preaching in the morning and then there is a usually a couple of hours between getting back home and going to the Kingdom Hall in the afternoon for the Sunday Service. Steve, as usual, had disappeared in the car while I got dinner ready. He was very late getting back for dinner and cutting it very fine to have time to eat and get back out again in time for the Service. When he got back, I could smell the drink on him again and he was in a bad mood about having to rush around so quickly. Steve wanted a clean pair of suit trousers for the meeting and I hadn't managed to get around to ironing the freshly washed pair. I was a lot more wary and frightened after how things had escalated before about where his mood could potentially end up, but despite the fact that I held back any opinion or backchat, the direction of the mood still hurtled out of control.

I went to fetch something from the car before we set off for the Kingdom Hall and that's where I discovered it. In the footwell in the back seats of the car was a woman's shoe. As soon I saw it, for some reason in my heart I just knew what it meant. What it was, was a sign of my worst nightmare.

I picked the shoe up and stormed back into the house with it and went straight up to Steve as he sat eating his dinner and placed the shoe on the table next to his plate. Steve face just changed as I saw the realisation in his eyes that he had immediately been put on trial.

Straight away an argument ensued. As the argument heated up, I could see the heat and rage in Steve build up. I could smell the couple of cans of lager he had drunk which spat in a near froth from his angry mouth. It didn't take too long before, once again, Steve lashed out at me and thumped me on the arm. Just as quickly again, he ran around the house, found another pair of trousers and ran out the house and into the car to the Kingdom Hall, leaving me drenched in tears and pain.

I could sense the pain coming from my arm was likely to produce another bruise, so I quickly got changed and put something on with longer sleeves. I wasn't going to miss the meeting this time and got out the house still in tears and started the long walk to the Kingdom Hall alone.

It was difficult to sit in the Kingdom Hall next to Steve and put a brave face on and pretend nothing had happened. Steve seemed to have no problem with it. He smiled, joked and waltzed around the Kingdom Hall, talking to people and shaking hands like nothing at all had happened. I played the faithful wife as well as best I could, but I felt a liar and a hypocrite, as though I was betraying my true self and concealing the truth from those around me.

Once the service was finished, the emotions filled up inside me for the two hours I was sat in that hall being the good wife, I had to seek out my friend Mary. I took Mary to somewhere quiet and out of the way and just burst out crying in front of her. I told her what had happened and showed her the bruises still on my ribs and now the one swelling on my arm and Mary was extremely shocked and taken aback. I told her about the woman's shoe that I had found in the car and how it answered my paranoia and suspicion.

It was only a couple of days later that I was then called in front of a group of Elders. I was being put on trial for bringing dishonour to my husband. At first I was confused, but it was explained to me that I should be supporting my husband, not gossiping about my husband's failings to other women in the congregation. I tried to explain to them what had been happening and showed the bruises to them and I pleaded with them for help. But the Elders insisted they couldn't tell a husband how to look after his family and that perhaps I should be more understanding of the stresses my husband was under. One of the elders promised to have a quiet word with Steve, but they told me that I was the one that should bring love back into our marriage.

I quizzed the Elders about the possibility that Steve is having an affair with someone and asked how I could stop his drinking and the problems that come from it. All the Elders told me was they were looking into the accusation and would be questioning Steve about both matters, but if Steve is in the wrong, then either God will punish him, or the Elders will deal with it, or failing that, Armageddon will solve my problem for me.

I felt so ashamed, emotionally bruised as well as physically and totally abandoned. Mary had obviously talked to her husband Ben. Ben then told the rest of the Elders and here we were.

The next couple of days were really difficult. Steve and I hardly talked to each other at home. At the Kingdom Hall he pretended that all was fine to the point that I felt physically sick whenever he put his arm around me like some tool to better his political standing.

After a few more days past, I realised that God had given me a duty to act responsibly for my husband and that the Elders were just my spiritual guides. I battled with myself to move my thoughts away from prejudice and conspiracy and looked towards Armageddon and getting back on track to make sure I would be saved from God's anger when the day finally arrived.

I eventually saw Mary again. She was partially apologetic but I could see the veil that always comes down when there is a conflict between faith and reason. I could tell that she wanted to help but knew there was a line and the Elders were the ones to decide where that line is drawn.

EVIDENCE 569832A
STEVEN MCPHEARSON'S DIARY

11TH JUNE 1975

What an awful couple of weeks. I am so angry with Anna. If I had any love left for my wife, it has been extinguished in these last couple of weeks. I know that I'm not a perfect husband and I am very aware that I am torn between the two lives that I am living, but Anna just jumps to conclusions and then spouts her mouth off at people about what is only our family business.

Anna found a shoe in my car. It didn't even belong to Julie, but it started off a massive row and a cascade of events that just flew totally out of control.

I've been dragged in front of a group of Elders in the congregation to answer a load of prying and personal questions. Ben wasn't allowed to be part of the group that questioned me. I knew the routine; I had been on their side of the interviewing panel. I suppose it gave me the opportunity to actually decide which of my two lives I wanted to live. The one with my wife and the faith or a short life in the open with Julie and then certain death at Armageddon. It's not much of a choice really, but I love Julie so much that I just cannot be apart from her. The stress of this double life is tearing me in two, but so far I've been enjoying both worlds. Great sex and love with Julie and at the same time power in the congregation.

Despite the fact that it was the obvious time to come clean and choose which life I wanted to live, I still held on with all my grit and determination to keep the status quo. I'm annoyed with myself that I still wanted both worlds.

Having been an Elder for a short while, I know how the game is played. I knew what to say to the panel and how to say it. I played the game and convinced them that there was no woman, I was having no affair and the violence against my wife was borne from the frustration of loving my wife so much. I played the game so very well that I was even convincing myself that none of my reactions where the fault of my own, but pressure from my stubborn and questioning wife.

The Elders decided I was truthful about not having another woman, but they did give me a stark warning about being violent against Anna and how I bring shame and reproach against the congregation when I let my anger get the better of me. But then they also told me that I needed to make sure that I keep Anna under control. What a contradiction that was.

They also quizzed me about drinking. I just enjoy a couple of light drinks every evening, I certainly don't go down to the pub every night and drink fifteen pints like many of my work colleagues do. That accusation really insulted me and I know it has put a huge dent in my chances of furthering my advancement up from an Elder. In fact, I know I was lucky to have not been stripped of being an Elder. The last few weeks have just been a complete hell and I have Anna to thank for that. All the work I have put in to get to where I am and now everything is in question because of her actions. I really do need to sort out these problems once and for all. I must get back on track, ha, and I must see Julie again.

Just thinking about Julie gets me excited. I'm going right now to see her....

EVIDENCE 569832C
TRANSCRIPT OF THE INTERVIEW WITH ANNA MCPHEARSON

13TH JUNE 1975

God does work in strange and unusual ways. On Friday and after just about getting some physical, emotional and spiritual strength back, the whole situation with Steve and I just accelerated again.

The final fight happened over something so small, pointless and trivial that I can't even remember what it was all about. As with every other time before, he had been drinking. This time it wasn't on a meeting night at the Kingdom Hall, so he had been drinking for most of the evening by the time everything went crazy. I wished that it had been a meeting night as at least there would have been something to divert the attention away to, somewhere he needed to go because this time he had all the time in the world to 'put me right' as he saw it.

It was an evening of sheer hell and despair. We started just arguing. I tried to remember my responsibilities and the advice I had been given by the Elders to be respectful by never raising my voice and attempting to calm the situation, but all that seemed to do was infuriate Steve even more.

The whole evening was bizarre. It was like being in a small boat on a twisting fast-flowing river. One minute there was calm and some serenity, then with just a bad look or an ill-toned word everything reared back up again into a froth and rush of adrenaline. Every time I tried and calmed the waters, it became futile as everything would blow back up again. As each moment passed, another can of lager was consumed and the next round of shouting got louder and more physically threatening.

At around 10pm, the threat of violence was getting very real and I had a sense of ever-nearing inevitability. I couldn't escape. I had nowhere to go, especially if the Elders had told me that this was my responsibility. I was shown from the Bible that I had a duty to my husband. I really did have no other way out of what seemed like an otherwise impossible path.

When the volume once again turned up, I had become powerless to stop the runaway events. I could sense that this time we had progressed to the next stage and Steve, so full of anger and rage, swung his fist at me with so much force that when it connected with the side of my head, it almost ripped off my ear.

I fell to the floor and almost lost consciousness. As I lay on the floor, dazed and confused, my ear whistled and numbed as the blood rushed out from my ear and over my face. The smell of the blood rushing into the carpet was the most unusual experience, a smell so strong I could almost taste the mix of iron and carpet fibre. Everything had gone silent and still. I wasn't in any pain, just strangely numb and light-headed. Lying on the floor almost felt like a strange dream; that I was experiencing this crazy scenario through someone else's experience.

It took some time lying there to realise where the voice was coming from just behind me. It was Steve. He had sat down on the settee next to my head and carried on drinking his lager and telling me how much I deserved my fate.

As I lay with the warm trickle of blood running down my face and soaking down into the carpet, the mumblings of my husband were barely discernible with my other ear.

The experience was surreal. After the loud, adrenaline rushed argument at the top pf our voices, there was a wonderful calm lying on that floor. I felt relaxed as though everything was slowing down in almost a slow motion film action. I honestly wondered if this was it, if this was the moment I was going to die. I was actually annoyed that if I was to die, I would miss Armageddon, that in the whole history of man, I lived in the moment that Armageddon was about to strike and I died just at the cusp of change. My mind had to go somewhere. Steve just sat mumbling to himself leaving me lying under his feet like I was the day's unfortunate prey.

I lay there for what seemed like an eternity, Steve drinking from the can of beer in his hand grinning and mumbling words I couldn't hear. Eventually he stood up, stepped over me still mumbling and drinking from the beer can, picked up his car keys and coat and left the house.

In the distance I could hear Steve get in the car, start the engine, pause for a few seconds then drive off at speed down the road. Then there was total peace and silence.

The blood flow from my head was starting to slow and congeal in my hair. Part of me wanted to stay where I was, go to sleep and wake up in the New World where I would be resurrected, the other part of me screamed to get up on my feet and get to the telephone and call for help.

As I lay warm, relaxed, dazed and calm on that soft carpeted floor, I could feel the world slipping away. This was to be my final moment, laying bloodied and broken, alone and dying on the living room floor by the hands of my husband. We hadn't even lasted a year of marriage. I thought about how God had answered my prayers. My problems were about to be resolved, just not the way I had anticipated or had desired.

It felt like an eternity that I was lying there, waiting for the end to come. I had no energy left to pick myself up from the carpet and get to the telephone. I could see a lake of my own blood crawling progressively longer and longer across the floor. The further it reached the closer I knew I was at an inevitable end.

I closed my eyes for one final time. I could feel the cold breath of death whisper over my dormant body. I said a prayer and said my goodbyes to God.

EVIDENCE 569832C
TRANSCRIPT OF THE INTERVIEW WITH ANNA
MCPHEARSON

14TH JUNE 1975

Dazed and feeling drunk from the blow to my head, I pulled every bit of energy I had left and gathered it all up for one final surge, one final attempt to move. I pulled my corpse up off the carpet and onto my knees and shuffled on hands and feet to the hallway to get to the telephone. As I crawled across the floor, blood dripping from the gash in my head, I couldn't think of who to call. Calling anyone would get them involved and I clearly remembered getting my friend Mary involved and how that worked out. It is amazing how many of my close friends and family had disappeared when I needed them, afraid to get caught up in the gossip and controversy. People I thought were close companions in the congregation that when it came to it, were just not there anymore. As a victim, I feared I was being tarnished as much as a perpetrator than a victim. Maybe it was because as the elders said, I was failing in my responsibility to resolve this myself with my husband.

This time I decided to try and get hold of Mary's husband Ben instead and go direct with the cry for help, straight to an Elder so that I wouldn't be spreading rumour and gossip. When Ben answered the telephone I just exploded with fear and tears, struggling in my dazed state and still feeling dizzy, to articulate what had happened. Once he realised the gravity of what was happening, he and his wife got in their car and quickly drove to my house to find me lying dazed on a carpet covered in my own blood.

Mary took care of me and started to clean up the carpet the best she could while Ben paced up and down mumbling to himself trying to think of what to do and how to proceed. Mary was so very caring, dabbing my head with a warm sponge while carefully watching her husband pace back and forth, both of us wondering what would happen. He suddenly stopped his pacing, looked at me and to my astonishment told me not to go to the hospital as Mary would take care of me that evening back at their house. Meanwhile he told me how concerned for Steve's welfare he was and said he was going to try a few places and have a go at finding him as he was troubled as to Steve's vulnerability.

I was dizzy, concussed, confused, physically and emotionally hurt and then to top it all off I felt betrayed and ignored. Mary gave me assurances and told me that we just needed to let God sort out these issues and that if we were faithful and we put trust in him, Jehovah will deliver us from our hardships.

Later, it was such a delight and relief to be at Mary's home. I felt warm and safe there and Mary really looked after me, cleaned me up and cooked a meal for me. I never saw Ben for the rest of the day. Mary looked after me for a few days at their house. She wouldn't let me lift a finger to help and just told me to lay around and spend my time recovering. She fed me and pampered me, and then after a few days, sent me home.

I returned to an empty house, to a blood soaked carpet and a fear of who may come home to me at any time. I decided to spend my time cleaning up the carpet the best I could and doing quite a bit of bible studying so as to keep myself busy and my mind occupied. It was Thursday and that night there was a meeting and I expected all day for Steve to come home and run around getting changed to go to the Kingdom Hall, but he never turned up. I walked to the Kingdom Hall on my own wondering where he was and why he shouldn't miss the meetings at such a crucial time before the onset of Armageddon. I was so glad that I had the day to myself and that Steve hadn't come home, but as the evening came, I got more and more anxious that he would turn up. I expected with every step of the walk to the Kingdom Hall that he would pass me in the car. Every engine noise I could hear behind me I thought might be his vehicle and every car that went past me was a relief. I wanted to see him, but not for the first time in the middle of a very public meeting.

I hesitated when I got to the Kingdom Hall and waited outside for a while. I couldn't see Steve's car in the car park, but I knew he had to be inside. A rush of anguish and anxiety swept over me as I felt paralyzed with fear, not wanting to go into the building. I just didn't know how to feel or how to act. I questioned who I was. I wanted to put on a brave front, but I strongly questioned who I was and how I naturally acted. I had never spent any time observing myself for this scenario. I had no idea who I was in order to be able to act the part.

I stood looking at the front entrance of the Kingdom Hall, fighting with myself to go in or to turn around and walk back home. Going home was likely just delaying the inevitable as Steve would go home at some point and we would still meet. At least there, in the Kingdom Hall, we were surrounded by people and so he was unlikely to get into an argument with me in public.

I was just on the verge of deciding that it would be best to go in and get it out of the way, when Mary appeared at the entrance, saw me and made a beeline for me. She grabbed my arm, put her arm around me and asked me how I was feeling and gently directed me in through the entrance. Mary told me not to worry, Steve wasn't there, which gave me such an instant relief to the point that I nearly collapsed from it. Then Mary also told me that I was exactly where I was meant to be as this was going to be one of the most important hours of my life.

I picked a quiet spot where I would be sat on my own. I sat myself down, tried not to make eye contact with anyone there and tried to focus on the meeting.

It was then at that meeting that from the platform it was announced what we had been waiting for so long. The Society had been watching world affairs closely. The withdrawal of US troops from Vietnam at the end of April had been the catalyst for the peace negotiated between North and South Vietnam. We had all been watching as the impossible seemed to happen and both sides manage to find a way of halting the fighting and begin negotiations.

The entire world had been looking on as America boasted of its power to resolve conflict against impossible odds. Every Jehovah's Witness looked on with different eyes though. We were all waiting for the signs that Armageddon was coming very soon, marked by two significant events predicted to happen before God's war would begin. The first would be a shout of "Peace and Security" from the great powers of the world, then those powers would turn on organised religion and try and shut them down. Then it was predicted that those same world powers would also turn on God's chosen people which would provoke Jehovah's wrath and then the end would come - Armageddon. This was the night when it would all begin. From the platform, it was announced that the Society had found out that the United Nations were about to declare its first state of world peace in just a couple of weeks' time and that this was going to set events in motion that would start the end of our times.

That announcement was like a bolt of lightning travelling down my spine. My head was still so sore and bruised, I was just not ready for that kind of shock on top of everything that had been happening. I couldn't help but think of Steve and the fact that he was missing this crucial and pivotal moment and I now actually wondered where he was from a point of concern. From the platform at the Kingdom Hall, amongst the mix of worry and excitement from the congregation, were instructions to start collecting belongings, essentials and food and bring them all into the Kingdom Hall by the weekend.

I began to feel a small amount of hope. God's kingdom on Earth was coming, the wickedness and injustice in the world would be a thing of the past and I would live forever in a paradise Earth if I survived the oncoming apocalypse. Part of me worried deeply that I might not be good enough, that I might not be pure enough to survive the coming test. God will destroy all those with an impure heart. I was still very confused about Steve. A part of me couldn't help but think that the fact that he wasn't there at the Kingdom Hall on such an important day could be God's justice and yet another part of me also thought that I didn't have the right to judge and that alone made me impure at heart and unfit for deliverance.

I was simultaneously excited and giddy and yet so very frightened, fearful of God's judgement and anger.

Everyone else in the congregation was also as confused emotionally as I was. In a way, there was a collective feeling of being blessed as we were the ones chosen to be there at the right place and the right time. We all had a sense of relief that now the time was eventually coming where we could all look forward to living a perfect life in a perfect paradise world. We could all see the panic in each other's eyes as well. That uncertainty cast a shadow through everyone that evening and already you could sense the wrong type of questions starting to creep in.

The congregation was told that over the next few weeks we all needed to prepare and be ready at a moment's notice for the call to rush to the Kingdom Hall. We will sit out the main war of Armageddon in the Kingdom Hall itself and we needed to all come together to prepare the Hall and ourselves for what was to come.

The usual Thursday night schedule had been thrown away and everyone become excited and cheered. We sang a half hour's worth of songs which filled everyone with a collective joy and spirit. Afterwards, everyone chatted and talked with enthusiasm and excitement and also nervous anticipation. I got so carried away with everyone actually talking to me and including me in a collective joy.

It took a long time for everyone to calm down and slowly filter away home. Ben and Mary offered to give me a lift home. Waiting for them to say their goodbyes to everyone for the evening just gave me time to come down from the high I had been on and my thoughts wandered back to wondering where Steve was and thinking that he might be back at home. When we finally got in the car, I killed the excitable talk stone dead by asking if anyone knew where Steve was.

Neither of them had heard or seen anything of Steve at all. I was surprised that Ben didn't seem the slightest bit concerned or bothered and I just got the feeling that he knew more than he was letting on.

We finally pulled up outside my home. Mary told me that I was going to be alone no more and from now on they were going to pick me up and take me to all the meetings. After a quick hug and goodbyes, Ben and Mary were gone and I was outside a dark and unlit house. Steve's car wasn't outside and it didn't look like he was inside either. The house was quite, lonely and cold. Steve was nowhere to be seen.

EVIDENCE 569832C
TRANSCRIPT OF THE INTERVIEW WITH ANNA MCPHEARSON

5TH JULY 1975

In two weeks I hadn't seen or heard anything of Steve. I knew that Armageddon was coming and it would arrive very soon, but the day-to-day worries of feeding myself and paying the bills were mounting lots of pressure on me that I just didn't need. Without any sign at all from Steve, the mortgage payments and utilities bills built up and I didn't have any cash to pay them with. I started to worry that I would be homeless and penniless way before the New Kingdom arrived.

Then at the Kingdom Hall I got word from someone that works at the same place as Steve that he had finally returned to work. He was well, and living a few miles away, although details were hazy at first about where and who with. I wrote a letter to Steve asking about getting some money for the bills as the house was under his name and I passed it to the Brother at the Kingdom Hall to pass onto Steve at work.

Steve wouldn't write a letter back to me; instead he just sent word that he would pay the house bills until I found somewhere else to live. He wasn't going to support me with food money; he passed on that it was up to me for find my own way for things like that.

I had to spend an age trying to find a way of getting welfare support from the government just to get some food. It was a nightmare. Even though I didn't want to, the welfare system was trying to push me down the legal divorce route in order to show that I was no longer dependent on my husband. But without a direct communication with Steve, I was struggling to get any resolve at all. Mary was a great help and she gave me bits of cash and food quite regularly. Although I was frustrated that I couldn't talk to Steve, it didn't stop me worrying that each evening he might turn up at home and we might start rowing and fighting all over again. Being on my own, and that constant threat of violence, was nerve racking and frightening. Add to that the perpetual need to watch for every piece of world news. On one hand I was desperate for Armageddon to just hurry up and arrive and on the other hand, like everyone in the congregation, I was nervous about whether I would make the grade; whether I was a good enough person to make it through.

The Elders decided that they needed to find out if Steve was committing adultery and be held accountable for it. It made me laugh and also made me quite sad that they wouldn't listen to me when it was me that brought it up, but then later they were all of a sudden interested again when they decided. The change in the world news and the fulfilment of prophecy that showed that Armageddon was imminent had speeded up plans in the congregation.

Whereas previously, each week would plod along with routine, habit and long term plans, everything changed to a sudden urgency to get things wrapped up, signed off and done before the real trouble started. The Elders interest in Steve was a typical example of that. Under normal circumstances it would likely take weeks and months to sort out these domestic issues, but the Elders had an urgency that was new as though they wanted things finished and finalised ready for the big day.

Then, just as the Society had announced, the world news was filled with a huge statement of the United Nations declaring worldwide "Peace and Security". For the first time since the birth of the United Nations, there were no active wars happening anywhere in the world. The peace brokered between North and South Vietnam, encouraged by the Americans and backed by the United Nations, was unprecedented. There was a huge swelling of public positivity to the point that it was becoming a little sickening. The news on every TV station, radio station and in every newspaper, declared how finally man had seen common sense and united the world for the greater good.

For all Jehovah's Witnesses around the world, it was a fascinating time to see and witness. It was difficult to not be swept up in the tide of love and happiness that the world celebrated as all Witnesses knew what the real consequences behind the headlines were. This was actually it. After 61 years of waiting for the first sign, it was actually arriving. Every Witness was now waiting for the next sign and wondering whether it would be days, months or years until the next step became apparent. The general consensus was that it was likely to be weeks rather than years. Tensions within the congregation were high. Each meeting at the Kingdom Hall was full of anticipation and sometimes drama, as accusations and finger pointing became regular habits. Everyone was both excited and very nervous at the same time and everyone looked around wondering who was going to fall away before the end came and who would be left standing faithful, into the New World.

It only takes another week before another announcement comes through from the Society that the United Nations were in talks with representatives from around the world about making worldwide changes to the way that religions present themselves and particularly the way they treat other religions. Although that was strictly not how the next phase of the prophecy was expected, it was accepted that it pointed towards being the next phase of Armageddon.

Everyone in the congregation was shocked at how quickly things seemed to be moving and the Elders asked that everyone stepped up in preparing the Kingdom Hall as a place of refuge for the whole congregation. Work started to be done to change the structure of the Kingdom Hall to make it more secure. Makeshift panels were made and put together to change the one big hall into lots of movable temporary rooms that were flat-packed and leaned up against the outer walls when the meeting was on. The smaller side room was now filling up with emergency food for doomsday. Many bottles of water, blankets and thousands of tins of food started to fill up the room, which was no longer to be used for meetings.

Every day there was a new fervour to get as much preaching work done as was humanly possible. When I was full time preaching, we met up twice a day to coordinate door to door knocking. Now, it was every hour and a half. Three weeks previously, everyone was just trying to act normal and carry on as usual, but now, people in the congregation were talking seriously about not going to work or stopping their children going to school to put effort into preparing the Kingdom Hall and going out preaching. Because of that new enthusiasm, new faces were showing up at the Kingdom Hall all the time. There was almost a controlled panic to save as many people as possible and bring them into the safety of the congregation.

That also caused some problems. Some families were desperate to trick loved ones into attending the meetings. There were some well-known former Jehovah's Witnesses that were showing their faces; some who had been ex-communicated or disfellowshipped from years previous. That started a whole debate about who should actually be let in at such a late stage and whether they deserved the forgiveness and opportunity to repent.

Tension in the congregation was building.

EVIDENCE 569832C
TRANSCRIPT OF THE INTERVIEW WITH ANNA MCPHEARSON

17TH JULY 1975

I've been spending little time at home recently. Nearly all my time has been taken up with either preaching work or working at the Kingdom Hall trying to get the hall prepared for the oncoming tribulation. There is little time to think. The Society has suggested we take up a more intense bible study regime to keep our minds occupied and prepare for what is to come. The Society has also been working tirelessly, printing new documents and leaflets, not just to give out on the preaching work, but also to give out guidance on what to do when the next steps in the prophecies emerge, with advice on how to best use the Kingdom Hall and how preparation works in the New World are being organised.

It all helps to build the excitement and also raises the tension as well.

I get word from Ben that the Elders have managed to

track down Steve and they are preparing to go and talk to him. As soon as Ben tells me, I start to wonder if Steve will change his mind and appear at one of the meetings. The thought partly makes me feel sick, which in turn makes me feel guilty. We are supposed to be forgiving and if Steve truly is sorry then he should be welcomed back into the congregation. But that raises so many questions and wild thoughts. What if he decides he wants his wife back; can I forgive him that much? What if he brings his new woman with him? At these close quarters, held up inside a sealed Kingdom Hall, that could be the worst idea of a transition to a New World that I could possibly think of.

Then of course, thinking so negatively also shows why I have to wonder if my heart is pure enough to be accepted into the New World or not.

I hear nothing from Ben or from Mary for over a week about Steve. Even though we spend a lot of time very close to each other, neither of them let a word of gossip slip. Eventually, as though it was inevitable, Ben took me to one side and sat me down. The Elders had met Steve and talked through what he wanted to do in great detail. Ben told me with great sadness in his voice and tears welling in his eyes, that Steve showed absolutely no repentance. Steve accepted that Armageddon was coming and that he was on the wrong side for what was coming at him at great speed, but he wanted to spend his last days with his new partner.

Ben then went on to say that Steve openly admitted to committing adultery and was facing the judgement of the Elders. Ben then passed on a message from Steve that he was sorry for what he had done to me and that I would finally be rid of him.

I didn't know what to make of the news. A part of me was glad, as though it was finally over. I was relieved that I was unlikely to see him again and that the threat of violence was likely gone, but I was also very sad and heartbroken. He was still my husband and I still loved him very much. I would have given anything to have the husband I married back with me.

The full horror of that news didn't really hit me until the next meeting. There, it was announced from the platform that Steve McPhearson was disfellowshipped and was no longer a Jehovah's Witness. There was a collective gasp in the Kingdom Hall that made me realise the true story that I had been ignorant to. Everyone turned around and looked at me with a mixture of bewilderment and pity. It was at that point that I realised that Steve's decision was going to cost him his life.

The next day Ben sat me down again and gave me some guidance that perhaps I may be relieved that Steve was going to accept a divorce. Ben then went on at some length to encourage me to refrain from looking for another husband until after Armageddon, when things will have settled down.

It was hard not to be really mad with Ben. I know that Steve and Ben were really close, but I really didn't want a divorce at all. I wanted the husband that I met and married a year before. I certainly didn't want Steve to be killed at Armageddon. I was grateful and relieved that the violence was going to stop, but I wasn't full of joy at losing my closest friend.

I also hadn't given a thought about looking for someone

else either. That was just typical of a man and thinking like a man. Men don't seem to be able to cope without having a partner. I certainly wasn't looking for anyone else. I needed time to get over this marriage first. Besides, with everything else that was happening around me, another person to look after was something I really didn't need.

Just as the Society had heard the rumours, the news in the newspapers and on the television was full of the talks between the countries of the world and the United Nations about how religions around the world should conduct themselves. It was announced that a new international law was to be observed, that while all religions had the freedom to worship what they wanted within the confines of their temples, churches and halls, it was to be neither moral nor legal to try and preach in public to others.

There were lots of public debates about how this new international law was to be enforced and how it was to be interpreted as well. It was generally agreed that television evangelism wasn't illegal because it was done in the confines of a virtual temple. A member of the public had to 'choose' to be involved in a television programme. It was also agreed that Muslim prayers over a loudspeaker and Christian church bells were calls to gatherings and not a public method of preaching, and were also not illegal.

Preaching in the street and from door to door however was clearly recognised as illegal and was therefore banned under the new international law. The Society immediately sent out word to all Kingdom Halls that this was the next fulfilment of prophecy; that the world governments would turn on religion and particularly Jehovah's people.

At first, nothing seemed to have changed, except for further renewed vigour to get the Kingdom Hall ready for war. Everyone became very serious and extremely focused. The Elders had discussed what to do about preaching. It hadn't taken very long at all for the UK government to pass a new law to ban public preaching. Strangely enough, within a day or so, it got through parliament and written into law. It was as though the government had been prepared for it and knew it was coming for quite a long time. The Elders decided that it was the most critical time to be saving lives and that the preaching work had to continue. Plans were drawn out and disseminated to all of us. We were only to preach to a few houses at a time and then move a few miles away. We could start again but had to just keep moving around. Everyone from the Kingdom Hall was starting to empty bank accounts, take out loans, even selling houses and putting cash into the Kingdom Hall funds. The plan was to use the cash, to not only stockpile food and to buy materials to upgrade the Kingdom Hall, but also to pay for legal bills to help keep people out of prison and get them back into the Kingdom Hall if caught preaching.

At first, when on the preaching work, we encountered no problems at all. It could have been that the police just weren't interested in us, or the plan to keep moving around was working well. By the time the police turned up anywhere, we were gone and had moved on elsewhere. But after a few days, a few of us had been picked up and arrested.

The Elders were desperate to make sure that when Armageddon came, one of us wouldn't be stuck in a police cell. Anyone who was caught and arrested - once bailed -

were not allowed out preaching again.

By the time some had been arrested, a few people had started to live in the Kingdom Hall. Some had sold their houses very quickly and had nowhere to live; others were working full time at the Kingdom Hall looking after the building, renovating it and getting it ready for the beginning of the end.

Tensions were high. There was a sense of inevitability, nervousness and excitement. The end was coming.

EVIDENCE 569832C
TRANSCRIPT OF THE INTERVIEW WITH ANNA
MCPHEARSON

21 AUGUST 1975

The past few weeks have been a period of crazy turmoil. Inevitably, I got caught preaching at someone's door when the police arrived. They arrested me and a friend. We spent the night in a police cell, which was frightening. Jehovah's Witnesses have become easy targets for general bullies, thugs and basically anyone with a tendency for violence. Being in a police cell was like being thrown into the centre of the devil's playground. Although we had no easy direct contact with the other inmates, at every opportunity we got covered in spit or were the direct target for verbal abuse and death threats.

I've had abuse from people when out on the preaching work before. It's a hazard of the job. I used to find the best way to tackle abuse was to try and face it head on and try to talk to them directly about God with sympathy and a human face. It nearly always worked, but in this circumstance I couldn't use that technique. We were strongly advised by the Society that if arrested for preaching, we would be wise to not preach at all to the police or to other prisoners, as such actions would jeopardise attempts at bail. It was a common sense approach I suppose, although we felt a moral duty to save everyone's life, but when committing an offence, the best defence is to stop offending.

We only spent one night in the police cell and then we were released but not allowed to leave the area. The courts were struggling with a hugely increasing backlog of arrests and cases that needed to go to court because of the new laws. It wasn't just Jehovah's Witnesses that were arrested, but thankfully because we all behaved when arrested; other more evangelical extremists were made priority for court appearances.

Because of my arrest, I had to stop preaching. I at least stopped it publicly. If I saw a friend or neighbour and stopped for a chat, I would try and steer a conversation around to what was happening around the world and to try and move the conversation towards a discussion about God. Some thought that was a little too dangerous and was against the spirit of the guidance given out by the Society, but if I saw someone I knew, I wanted the chance to save their lives. Besides, the job of preaching was actually getting easier. Strange things were happening around the world. The newspapers were full of reports of unusual worldwide random deaths that defied logic and sense. There were reports from NASA that the Sun was going through a very unusual phase of activity that all the scientists around the world were arguing and speculating about as to what was actually happening and what the likely impact would be on the Earth over the coming days and weeks. Every time we saw another headline in the newspapers, we all knew in the congregation what it meant and what was really happening.

The atmosphere in the congregation was a mix of excited anticipation and raw fear. A meeting would take several hours instead of the usual two, because everyone just wanted to sing songs to boost our hopes and quash our fears. New faces were showing up daily at the Kingdom Hall to the point that every evening, there had to be new sermons and meetings just to allow everyone to be involved. Bible studies were held all day with new people which became a fast track to enrolment. The Kingdom Hall became a full time open house. There was never a minute of the daytime that something wasn't being done, either in the building work, the accruing of supplies, bible study groups or singing groups. At night, the hall would be turned into dormitories using the newly built panels and people would sleep there overnight.

There were also many shock announcements being made regularly by the Elders, of people being punished, disfellowhipped or banned from the Kingdom Hall. It was almost a whipped up frenzy of accusations left, right and centre. The Elders had a full time job on their hands just going through one hearing after another regarding accusations of adultery, fornication, apostasies, thefts and violence. I could tell that the pressure of the onset of Armageddon had made some go mad with fear and anxiety, and started to act in ways totally out of character; ways that they would never have acted under any other circumstance. There were times when I thought that perhaps the Elders had gone too far with their punishments. After all, the decisions they were now making were life or death sentences for individuals. All I could do was put my faith in God that his appointed Elders in the congregation and in the Society were making the right choices. There were many times that I really started to wonder, but I myself was fearful of questioning at such a crucial point in time.

There became a growing spirit of fear against the Elders in the congregation and the potential power of life and death they now wielded over everyone. Of course, to say anything out loud would be to invite an accusation of apostasy and damnation. No-one questioned their authority; nobody dared to.

The situation at home was growing ever more desperate. Every few weeks I would receive a cheque in the post to cover the mortgage and for a few other essential bills from Steve. Apart from those cheques, I would hear or see nothing of Steve at all. He never even called at the house to check anything. For all he knew, I could have burnt the whole place down. I strongly suspected that he saw what was happening in the news and knew himself that this was the end, and so he was likely making the most of it with his new partner. That was my assumption.

I was becoming busy and was so focussed on the Kingdom Hall that I was neglecting the house that Steve owned. I still went home every evening and slept there. I sometimes ate breakfast in a morning, but that was about all I saw of the house. There was never any sign at all that Steve had been there, week in week out. I lost focus on the domestic duties completely. Letters had started to arrive in the post with red lettering and the words "final demand" on them. I just didn't give anything at home any priority next to what was happening at the Kingdom Hall every day, to the point that it was getting close to losing the house completely. I wasn't cashing Steve's cheques or paying the bills and the fact that Steve never turned up to question anything just re-enforced to me what I was suspecting. Steve was making the most of the time he had left.

Then the weather started to get very strange. We had snow in August, then a week later record heat. At night, the midnight sky would glow purple, pink and green. The newspapers were full of stories about unusual spots on the Sun and massive flare eruptions, and still everyone in the scientific community were baffled about what was happening. We would hear of random and sudden deaths occurring in the local area, as though a symptomless plague had broken out. People of all ages would just randomly drop dead in the street. The whole country had an air of anger against the government and the scientific community seemed as clueless as everyone else as to what was happening.

It was amongst all this, that one Thursday evening there was a major announcement from the Kingdom Hall platform. Ben had an envelope from the Society headquarters in London with strict instruction not to open until that Thursday evening on the 21st August 1975 at exactly 8pm UK time, and to read it out to the congregation. All through that day, everyone knew about that letter and speculation was rife as to what it might be.

The atmosphere in the congregation that evening at exactly 8pm was terrifying. Ben stood on the platform nervously with his fingers shaking, trying to open the envelope. The colour of the sky through the high slit window in the walls shone a psychedelic mix of purples and greens through the glass onto the platform, as though God himself had decided to make the announcement all the more dramatic.

Ben eventually ripped open the envelope and took out the professionally folded letter. He paused as he opened the folded paper and started to silently glance down at its contents as everyone in the packed hall stared in absolute quiet, waiting for Ben to read out the contents.

I could clearly see tears welling up in his eyes as he took off his glasses and looked out over the waiting crowd. Everyone could see him physically shaking as he brought the paper back up to his face and put his glasses back on. Mary could see how shaken Ben was and jumped up onto the platform, grabbed his arm and held his spare hand tightly.

Ben read out the letter. It announced to everyone, that the following Sunday the 24th August 1975, all that wished to be saved from the oncoming Tribulation and Armageddon were to bring everything that they had gathered and bring it to the Kingdom Hall, along with all their loved ones that also wished to be saved. The Kingdom Hall doors were to be shut and locked for the last time on the old world at strictly 8pm that evening and all who weren't inside the Kingdom Hall by then would be left outside, would perish and would not be saved.

Everyone gasped out loud in shock and terror. People started to cry and some rejoiced and praised God loudly. It was such a bizarre and mixed response from everyone. All I could think about was Steve, the journey that had brought me there, lying on that living room floor bleeding to death and being so very thankful and grateful that Steve and I had decided not to have children.

EVIDENCE 569832C
TRANSCRIPT OF THE INTERVIEW WITH ANNA MCPHEARSON

3RD OCTOBER 1975

Everyone was rushed, frantic and panicked over those next few days to get the Kingdom Hall finished for a couple of hundred people to live in for an undisclosed amount of time and to get those that could be convinced to drop their lives entirely and come and barricade themselves inside the Kingdom Hall with the rest of us.

There were surprisingly few non Jehovah's Witnesses that did. Even with all the strange news and weather occurrences happening, we must have all looked like a bunch of crazy religious zealots or a mad cult all ready to commit mass suicide inside a homemade bunker.

It was very heart wrenching to see people in the congregation with families that were not Jehovah's Witnesses upset because they were unable to convince their loved ones of what was coming. It was extremely upsetting to see the hurt in my Brothers and Sisters as they sometimes physically tried to drag them against their will to the Kingdom Hall.

Most of my blood family lived across the country. I had telephone conversations with them and they told me that they were prepared, safe and would be ok. That was a huge relief and allowed me to concentrate on getting myself and my friends prepared for what was to come.

Those three days disappeared so quickly. It was no time at all from when the announcement eventually came to closing the doors to get everything done that we all thought was necessary. We had no idea of how long we were going to be held up inside the Kingdom Hall, so we didn't know how long the provisions would last. Our designated area that the congregation covered was on the edge of a city. It included an area of thousands of homes and tens of thousands of people. When the Sunday morning came around, there were barely a hundred people gathered in the Hall. As the day progressed - although there was a steady stream of people turning up with belongings, camp beds, stoves, canned food stuffs, blankets and clothes - the numbers were still small.

I was kept very busy helping people find an allocated space in the cramped Kingdom Hall, guiding them to facilities and helping them get some food. The Elders were very organised and had everyone given a particular job in order to keep people occupied. Some looked after food distribution, others organised bedding and blankets, while some entertained children and a few organised prayer corners and a listening ear as well as counselling. There were groups of men still hammering, sawing and building away at makeshift boxes and moveable walls. It was all a mixture of chaos and purpose at the same time.

By the late Sunday afternoon of August 24th 1975, there weren't even two hundred people in the Kingdom Hall and the number of people trickling in had started to slow considerably. I was really struggling with the numbers. All I could think about was the tens of thousands of people that I and my congregation had a responsibility for. Why couldn't we convince them? Why had we failed so badly? I thought of my neighbours. I thought of the people I regularly sold The Watchtower to. Even the people I had bible studies with were not there. Finally, I thought about Steve. It was Steve who was at the forefront of my mind and heart when at 8pm exactly, the outer doors of the Kingdom Hall were slammed shut!

That was it. There were no more to be admitted under any circumstances. The doors were closed and this was finally the end. Four Brothers started to nail thick pieces of timber across the main entrance doors on the inside. Then, as if to prove a point, the secondary inner doors were also shut, locked and nailed shut with an applause of hammer bangs. Large pieces of painted black out boards that had been specially prepared were then heaved up to the small, high windows around the main hall. Within a half hour, all the banging, clattering and hammering had stopped and we were all silent in a darkened hall. For a half hour under the artificial neon tube lights, nobody talked as Elders and Ministerial Servants quietly gathered themselves and read through the plans and instructions they had been given between them.

Then one of the Elders stood up at the platform and explained what we were to do for that first evening. First, there was a lecture taken from a specially prepared talk posted in by the Society which took an hour. Then, we went through a half hour of prayers and singing. That helped lift spirits a little from the air of nervousness that was colouring the room. Finally, there was guidance about how everything was going to be organised - at least over the first few days. No-one was allowed into the building from the outside under any circumstances from then on. There would be volunteers put to work on different duties such as food preparation, cleaning, changing the hall around for its different functions, store keeping, security etc . There were rules on curfew and what the daily routine was going to be. There would be prayers each morning, afternoon and evening, with bible studies and readings every evening. Even makeshift improvised children's plays would take place - on bible themes of course.

Once the planned proceedings had completed on that first night by just after 10pm, the first curfew was put into place. The main hall was moved around, the makeshift panels were brought in and quickly put into place as planned and several dorm rooms were created ready for people to sleep. We had all been kept busy that day and by 11pm the lights were being turned down and the whole Kingdom Hall settled into a troubled and nervous night.

I could hear the Elders still chattering quietly away in specially designated corner of the hall, making their plans and setting up itineraries. Although we were supposed to sleep, we could all tell that it would be a very difficult night to rest. Everyone had their ears tuned towards the world outside. Once everything was quiet inside, it was as though nothing was happening outside. We could hear traffic as usual - the odd typical city noises, a shout, the banging load of a passing lorry. The lack of anything sinister just helped make the tension even worse inside the hall. Although none of us knew what was going to happen outside, we all expected the noise of earthquakes, explosions and the like, right from the off. The general quiet of everyday life became a little unnerving.

When we all awoke in the morning and got busy moving the temporary panels back to the side walls to open up the hall once again, there was talk between everyone as to whether they thought anything at all had happened outside. The first scheduled morning prayers took place and we all started to ask around if anyone was going to look outside to see if anything at all had changed. It only took an hour of people asking questions for those questions to reach the ears of an Elder and a public announcement was called. One of the Elders took to the platform and warned us all that nobody was to make any attempt to look outside no matter how curious they were. We were reminded of the story of Sodom and Gomorrah and how Lot's wife, who stopped to look back at the burning city, was turned into a pillar of salt. We were told that under no circumstance were we to let curiosity or regret take us to an untimely end.

It was difficult though to stop the gossiping and speculation. Some were concerned that they had been duped into holding up in this building while their houses were likely being looted and ransacked. All day we could hear from outside nothing but typical city traffic; all the noises we came to expect from living near the city. There wasn't even a telephone in the Kingdom Hall. There was never any need for one generally and in the rush of sudden panic, there hadn't been any time given to get a line fitted in the space of a week. Ben told me that although the postal service may try to put letters through to the Kingdom Hall, the letterbox had been nailed shut, which was one of the instructions from the Society. Once those doors were closed, they were not to be opened.

The normality didn't last too long though. It was only on the second evening that we could hear children outside taunting us and shouting abuse and laughter at us all closed up inside the Kingdom Hall. We could hear the thuds and smashes of bottles and objects being thrown at the building. It was obvious that word had got around that we were held up inside, much to the amusement of what eventually sounded like a large gang of thugs and kids outside. Thankfully, nothing was seriously broken on the building and when the evening service started, our singing blocked out some of the shouts and taunts. After a couple of hours they became bored from getting no reaction from anyone inside and had moved elsewhere.

On the third day, there was still no sign of anything unusual coming from outside and many started to wonder what we were doing held up like sardines in the relatively small Kingdom Hall. The lights still worked, the PA still allowed music to be played and the microphones to work from the platform. Water still ran from the taps and the toilets still flushed. It was obvious that outside the building, the city infrastructure was still intact.

By the fourth and fifth days, gossip had turned into heated opinion and some were openly denying that anything at all was happening outside and that we had all been lied to and deceived. The Elders struggled to contain the open rebellion being led by just a few people, noticeably ones that weren't actually Jehovah's Witnesses themselves, but relatives that had been persuaded to join us.

By day six, there was a very real threat of the breakdown of order and discipline. A band of about fifteen insisted that they be let out of the building or they promised that they would get violent. The Elders decided, against the rules that they were given, that in order to save the majority, we would have to let those defiant few leave the Kingdom Hall. It was a difficult task to accomplish. The inner doors had to be freed and then the outer doors were only worked on by two Elders to get them open, both of whom went to great lengths to make sure they didn't even chance a glimpse at the outside world during the very brief moment that the outer doors were slightly opened to allow those who wished to leave, to go. We all heard the frantic work to shore up the doors again once they had gone, and to make sure they were blocked up even more solidly than before.

It was on the eighth night that we were all quiet and demoralised. I think everyone was wondering if they should have asked to be able to leave. I know I doubted and questioned if I was right to stay where I was. It was just before the evening sermon started that a new noises were heard outside the building. First there was an almighty crash, as though a couple of vehicles on the road had collided, which was followed immediately by screams of terror and shouting. It got the notice of everyone in the hall. We all waited as a period of silence followed, everyone wondering what the crash was. In the silence, I speculated that it was just a road accident and we were all making more of it because we were expecting so much more. It was then that there was a huge explosion outside and the whole building shook for about twenty seconds. For a moment, the lights all dimmed and we all held onto each other, while looking around the hall waiting for another sound.

For the next half hour, there were screams of terror and loud arguments coming from the outside. That was followed by shouts and sirens of emergency vehicles stopping nearby. We were supposed to have started the service, but because not even the Elders could do anything except listen to the sounds from outside, the service just didn't happen. Although the noises stopped after a couple of hours, we all struggled to sleep even in the quiet of the night.

Each day then escalated from there. More huge explosions, crashes of sound, the building shaking and the lights flashing. It was as though earthquakes, storms and stampeding elephants were all fighting to make the most noise outside the building.

The whole commotion made me withdraw within myself. I battled with both my thoughts and my heart. I was so scared that God would know what I was thinking and feeling and that I would be violently plucked from out of the hall and thrown in a bloody mess into the world outside. These feelings I was trying to supress were ones of shame and guilt. I knew it was wrong, but I couldn't help thinking about the billions of people outside the hall being tortured and violently mutilated. I was safe inside at that moment, but I questioned in my heart if all those people deserved what they were being put through. If only Jehovah's Witnesses were to survive, how were most of them outside the Kingdom Hall really given any chance to make a choice?

I had tried to reach as many as I could; tried to get them to open their eyes, to see and fear what was coming. But I could see that out of hundreds of people I would talk to, only one would show any interest at all. I didn't blame them for their disinterest. Jehovah's Witnesses have a reputation and it doesn't help when trying to approach people. Those questions just kept going through my head, sending me insane. We didn't really reach anyone at all in the great scheme of things. No-one really listened and is that enough to kill them for it? Their ignorance wasn't malicious. How can the killing of the whole human race - except for a few million - be justified when hardly anyone got a chance to know how to avoid this awful fate?

I was also guilty by association. Yes, God was killing those billions of people outside the Kingdom Hall, but I and my fellow worshippers, by following God and accepting what he was doing, are complicit in this genocide. I couldn't help but recall the German people of the 1930s who pleaded that they did not know what was happening to their neighbours and tried to clean that guilt away when actually they knew deep down of their guilt of silence. Our collective Brothers and Sisters were guilty of not standing up and saying NO. I was guilty. I felt that shame and I tried to hide it from my thoughts and from my heart.

I feared a fate worse than death. Only a Jehovah's Witness would know that fear. Death is just an end; a completion into nothingness. But to be shamed by disapproval from God and the Elders is worse than death, because you then spend eternity in God's displeasure. In death, you become nothing and if you're really fortunate, someone might remember you. But to spend an eternity being one of those that God despises - and that every Christian for eternity will also despise as a wrongdoer and evil - is worse than a simple death into nothing. I feared that fate greater than death itself, so I fought with myself. I fought with my emotions and I tried to hide from God.

From the outside of the Kingdom Hall were the continual blood-curdling screams. Sounds of human terror and pain that turned your blood cold. As each day went by, a new way of crying in anguish would be heard outside that would put a shiver through everyone in the hall. It was at the end of the second week that we first had people outside banging on the main entrance doors, shouting and pleading to be let inside. The horror of those voices would haunt us every night as we tried to sleep. Some of us pleaded to the Elders to let some people in - the ones outside that had the stamina to bang on the doors for hours, crying and pleading for God's mercy and to be let into the building. At one point I even thought in a half sleeping nightmare state that I heard Steve's voice outside shouting my name. The Elders were very clear and firm. No-one was allowed in or out, or even to talk to those shouting outside the building.

On the fourth week, someone inside the Kingdom Hall suddenly died in the night. It was very creepy. They seemed healthy and fine in the day. They were relatively young and fit, but the next morning they weren't breathing and had turned stone cold. There was no sign of ailment - or of anything sinister - just a natural death with no explanation. That very much put everyone in the Kingdom Hall on a new level of anxiety. It seemed that even though we had made the sanctuary of the building, it didn't necessarily mean we would be successful in getting through to the

New World.

Eventually at the start of the fifth week, all the amenities failed. First the electric, then the gas heating, then the water and sewage system all failed within a couple of days. We spent each evening under candle and paraffin lamp light.

It was in the fifth week that the noises from outside became fewer and fewer until midway through week five, outside was totally silent all day and all night. The silence was worse than the blood curdling screams and deathly terrors. We all knew what it meant. Day after day we had a complete silence except for the sounds within the Kingdom Hall. Despite all the plans to keep busy, the silence shocked us all into long bouts of contemplation. We all knew that silence had been paid for by billions of human deaths.

Our collective thoughts then started to move on to what we were going to see once we got outside. God had promised us a New World; a perfect paradise after the tribulation of Armageddon. There was rife speculation as to how the outside would be cleared and cleaned up for us to enjoy the promise of a paradise Earth. Many speculated that a flood may have cleared the Earth or even rivers of magma and crazier theories did the rounds in the overcrowded hall.

It was on the evening of the 3rd October 1975, that the Elders told everyone in the Hall that it had been forty days since that Sunday when we locked ourselves in the Kingdom Hall. The Society had given out the instruction that on the first morning after the 40th night, we were to exit the Kingdom Hall and go back out into the open. We all rejoiced and sang hymns for the entire night. Everyone was praising God and thanking the Elders for looking after us all. We had made it. We had all survived Armageddon.

TRANSCRIPT OF THE INTERVIEW WITH ANNA
MCPHEARSON

YEAR ZERO, DAY ZERO OF THE NEW SYSTEM

I cannot begin to explain to you the shock and absolute disappointment I felt when I emerged from the Kingdom Hall on that first day, but I will try.

After being shut away for 40 days and 40 nights, locked up in a small Kingdom Hall with nearly two hundred other people, with no natural light, practically no fresh food left and nearly a week spent with no running water and the sewage system backed up, we were all eager to get outside and enjoy some fresh air, fresh food and curious to see our new paradise home.

Everyone was in a strange mood. Some of us found it easy to ignore the obvious, but many including myself were hoping that this new world would be worth the billions of lives that had paid for it. I was in a mixed mood, realising that I had been party to the genocide of the whole human race. The fact that I was right there at the moment we were about to open those doors made me part of the responsibility of those billions of deaths. That feeling was combined with the purely selfish eagerness to enjoy its reward. If I was to be guilty, at least it had to be in an ignorant bliss of paradise.

The inner doors were practically mauled apart in the enthusiasm to get outside. All of us converged in a surge of bodies waiting to get through the doorway and see what we had all inherited.

In one crash of splintered wood and nails, the external double doors of the Kingdom Hall flew open and the waft of external air drew in quickly and rushed into the hall. We all stood and took a deep breath and - collectively - nearly all choked.

How do I describe the stench of a collapsed civilisation and the rotting, putrid decaying smell of four billion human bodies and countless billions of animal carcasses? That is what began to fill our lungs in a rush to get out of the Kingdom Hall. We didn't need to see anything at that point; all of it was apparent through our noses. I actually wanted to go back into the hall; I preferred the dank smell of two hundred live bodies and not what greeted me outside.

For what seemed like an eternity, everyone stood still and shocked in the grounds of the Kingdom Hall. No-one had anticipated what lay in front of us, except perhaps the Society. As soon as the shock had lifted, the Elders started distributing work allocations to everyone. I went and talked to Ben who showed me another envelope from the Society that had been sealed until that day. In it, the letter described how all of us as survivors needed to create a base and a network connection established and from there further instructions would come. The Elders quickly gave out instruction to send someone to the next nearby Kingdom Hall and create a line of communication.

It was apparent that there was no road structure left. The Kingdom Hall was surrounded on all sides by mounds of piled dirt, rubble and devastation. Two men were assigned network duty to go and talk to the people at the next Kingdom Hall some miles away and then to report back to us. The Elders also gave out roles to everyone, roles based on the guidance in the letter from the Society. Some roles made sense, such as making sure people had food, shelter and fresh water. But some roles were very unusual. I was put on body duty. Body duty was one of two outside-facing jobs. One was to be back-breaking work clearing rubble, concrete, bricks, glass and all the destruction that lay around the Kingdom Hall and the other duty was body duty, clearing up pieces of human and animal flesh and burning the remains.

How much further that was from the paradise Earth I had expected after Armageddon could that reality actually be? I didn't feel rewarded, I felt punished. This was to be my penance for the combined responsibility of four billion deaths. I chose the side of Genocide.

The very first time I was told that I was on Body Duty, it took a couple of hours begging with the Elders that I couldn't physically do it. To pick up bits of human and animal bodies and put them into wheelbarrows at first just made me vomit over and over again. But the Elders told me that first of all I would quickly get used to it and adapt and secondly, being in the New World, my body was now perfect. I wouldn't get ill or sick ever again, so the vomit reaction would become less and less as my imperfect body moved and healed into a perfect state.

Day by day, it got easier, but it didn't help my state of mind at all. There were quite a few people that were seriously questioning if this New World was right or wondered if the Elders had made a huge mistake. Some of us wondered if the perfect paradise we had been promised was actually some hundreds of miles away and it was just going to be a matter of time until the Society found all of us and rounded us up and took us there.

It was only a week or so of burning thousands of rotting, smelly, ripped up body parts that a new face turned up at the Kingdom Hall. The network had been a success and a travelling overseer from the Society was doing a tour and updating Kingdom Halls on the next steps needed.

There was a renewed excitement that at last a spokesperson of God was here to show us the way to paradise. He arrived in the morning and the whole of the congregation was gathered for his address that afternoon. From there he would be moving onto the next congregation that evening.

His address was not the relief everyone was expecting. "Armageddon had gone and we were God's chosen few that survived to be perfect and live forever in his paradise Earth" - that was his message. It was in the detail that many of us felt cheated. We had an eternity to attain paradise. God never promised a time limit. God also never promised to do all the work for us either. The overseer explained that we had a duty to God; to clear the wicked from the Earth. It was our job to clean up the mess and create the paradise that we all yearned to live in. The Elders were our chosen guides and they would organise the work to return God's Earth back to a paradise.

EVIDENCE 569832C
TRANSCRIPT OF THE INTERVIEW WITH ANNA MCPHEARSON

YEAR THIRTY, DAY 245 OF THE NEW SYSTEM

I have spent more than thirty years cleaning up death, rot, disease and filth from the land around the Kingdom Hall. Although I get more and more used to it, there is something inside my head and heart that can never stop struggling with the guilt of what it is I have spent all this time doing.

I now have a daily routine of getting my days cleaning area assignment from Ben. He co-ordinates the clean up around the Kingdom Hall catchment area. We have met some of the surrounding area congregations a few times where our boundaries meet. It seems that progress is as slow everywhere as it is in our region. We have hundreds of square miles to cover and although the Body Duty unit has cleaned up about 10 percent of the region, the Rubble Duty unit still haven't cleaned up 2 percent of the region.

No matter how efficient I become at clearing out the body parts and ignoring the wretched decay, or ignoring the smell in the evening of all that flesh burning on the pyre, I still have many a moment that stops me and makes me question everything. I've found bodies of children, whole families burned huddled together in their house, a corpse of a pregnant woman killed halfway through a birth. All these are time capsules of the Great Armageddon, the cleansing of all these evil wicked people.

I just cannot help myself and wonder what could have been so evil about these people that they deserved to die like that. There are quite a few of us that have feelings that we have been easily duped into thinking the wrong thing, feeling like an idiot for not seeing what now seems blatantly obvious. Because I never stood up and said that this should not be done, I have to take a responsibility for that choice. I, and some of my colleagues, struggle very much to come to terms with the fact that surely all 4 billion people killed 30 years ago were not all evil rampant murdering sinners that deserved what they got. As a bystander, as someone who benefitted from that action and said nothing to declare that it should not be done in my name, I am as guilty of those 4 billion deaths as if it were my hand and not God's that did the killing.

A lovely man - a good soul - was set to work with me on Body Duty. We have worked for 30 years together and we completely confided in each other. Initially, after Armageddon, normal ways of previous living were resumed. But soon, the Society took over many aspects of social order and new laws. As we all became perfect in body and because now we would never die of any disease or old age, new rules and social etiquettes were seen to be needed. So, relationships between a man and a woman have to be approved centrally by the Elders and children have to be planned and approved. There is a concerted effort to make sure that the earth is not overcrowded and everything is managed centrally and properly.

It leaves the Elders in great centres of power locally. Some couples are afraid to mention to the Elders and therefore publicly any romantic interest in case the Elders do not approve and split couples up. The two of us keep our feelings between us in fear we may be split up. We don't do anything about it, just sometimes talk about what life would be like if we were married, if we had children, what names we would call them, all those kind of sweet things. It was nice to actually feel love for someone again. He was nothing like Steve at all which made everything about him so fresh.

We were on the verge of taking the next step and going to the Elders and asking permission to couple together and get married, but before we could, a new ruling came from the Society.

It came through only last week. The Society decided that because full population management was required in the New World and because everyone was going to live together, marriage had become obsolete. Only the production of children by approval was now the sacred task in the New Order. No-one would get married, but twenty year couplings would be allowed and approved. No marriage would take place and couples would be required to part from their union after the set period of time and either stay single or look for a new coupling.

As a Christian brought up with the sanctity of marriage, I really struggled with all of the new rules. Apart from the problems of conscience, formed over many years with one set of specific rules, I couldn't help but fear the loss of many freedoms. Many choices and previous freedoms were being taken away or controlled which was the opposite of what I expected. I always thought of freedom and free will to be trait of God. When man was created in God's image, it was always taught to me that it was the freedom of choice that made us God-like.

I have fought with myself more and more over my conscience and the realities of this New World. If I question this New World, then surely I am questioning God himself. The Society keeps making it clear that to question the Elders or to question the rules and laws of the Society is to directly question God, which is the worse sin. It is apostasy.

Was I becoming an apostate after everything I had been through and witnessed?

EVIDENCE 569832C
TRANSCRIPT OF THE INTERVIEW WITH ANNA MCPHEARSON

YEAR EIGHTY ONE, DAY 78 OF THE NEW SYSTEM

I still can't get used to being over a hundred years old. I know I was born into the family of what used to be known as Jehovah's Witnesses and I always believed that I could see a time when death would be no more, yet it's still mind blowing to not grow old or not have ailments. I still look the same as I did eighty one years ago, although I suspect that experience shows in my eyes.

Our congregation is so close to finishing Body Duty. I run a team of about twenty. All are good hard working people. We all find the work upsetting although the years of decay mean we see less and less flesh these days and mostly bones now. But still, the hard work to clear our congregations appointed catchment area has nearly come to an end. I wish I could say the same for the Rubble Duty teams who still have so much work to do even though they have such a large team. I suppose it doesn't help that the new housing projects take people from the Rubble Duty roster.

Eighty years and still we aren't living in the paradise we thought we were going to live in. There has been a lot of work done though and a great deal has been accomplished.

After my first coupling being childless, I didn't feel the need to start another coupling, so I've stayed single for the last thirty years. I still feel so very uncomfortable with many aspects of the New World. There are so many erosions of free choice and as time passes it becomes more and more obvious how political and unequal everyone actually is. There has been a renewed effort to expand on a home building project around the country, yet there is little stimulus to back the project anywhere. Most Elders have all had homes designated to them for decades now, many of them very large, well looked after and beautifully styled. It is hard not to think that the greater the political influence the more that influence is reflected in the homes of those people.

I am not coupled and neither do I have children. I am a Duty Leader of the most despised Duty work that can be assigned and of course I am a woman and as such I have no right to anything, including politics, social funding or any meaningful leadership roles. I am invisible and as such will be one of the last to ever get a home of my own.

I suppose in a way it's my own fault as I have so far chosen not to couple with anyone or have children either. I still battle with my conscience, as do a lot of the older people that still remember the old world. The older generation are also seen by the younger as being less educated and useful. Back in the old world, we were told to keep away from higher education and from further education. This meant that many of our kind had a lot fewer skills than those born in this New World. They are taught many practical skills that can be used to build the paradise we have all been after for these many decades.

It seems that I am not the only one to carry the guilt of the genocide of the old world. Over the years I have heard many from that old world express the conflict that creates a great turmoil within themselves, just like the issues I have felt, especially spending all this time cleaning up the thousands of bodies that I have had to burn and destroy. Many also share my worries about the corrosion of free will. I think the Society have sensed this and so have been moving to appoint more Elders from the new generation, and are trying to water down the older influence of the Elders from the old world. The newer generation have such a different viewpoint of matters such as free will and choice and are a lot more strict and disciplined. They can also be reckless and without caution. They have never known common death, disease, pain and aging. They also have never known imperfection and expect everyone and everything to be right and perfect first time and every time for always. There is an absolute zero tolerance expectation from all of them.

My generation of people from the old world are being ostracised and there is a growing movement and atmosphere to resist. It bubbles quietly just under the surface, always.

EVIDENCE 569832C
TRANSCRIPT OF THE INTERVIEW WITH ANNA
MCPHEARSON

YEAR NINETY EIGHT, DAY 21 OF THE NEW
SYSTEM

There has been a heart-breaking change in attitude from the Society over the last decade or so. The international network of communication has been established and perfected in the last few years and now there is one central source of guidance from God that updates everyone across the Earth in real time, something we hadn't had since Armageddon when the existing infrastructure was destroyed.

Now regular publications keep us up to date with the co-ordinated effort to build our paradise Earth and also keep everyone in line with the rapidly changing laws and rules handed down from the Society.

It is late summer here and we have just celebrated the 98th Anniversary since climbing out of that Kingdom Hall into the New World, although in my cynicism, the promise of a New World paradise is only just starting to be realised. It has been and continues to be back-breaking work. There is still little in the way of the modern technologies that we once took for granted. Without the greed of commerce or war to drive improvements and advancements in technologies, technological evolution is slow and cumbersome.

We are kept busy. I think that it is a basic driver from the Society. Without the preaching work, which used to take up all our time a hundred years ago, there is a danger of sitting around and thinking too much, so we are kept praying, singing, studying and working at a full time and exhausting rate. Everyone is so tired all the time that we hardly notice the changes being made bit by bit, year by year.

To demonstrate exactly what I mean I only have to think back three weeks ago to the 98th local celebrations. The heart of the local celebration was around a large collection of wood made into a bonfire-shaped mound with three tree trunks firmly structured and set upright. I had heard rumours of similar occurrences happening around the country from some of the older people like myself who were really struggling to understand what was happening and what we were working towards.

Three young men were brought to the party gagged and bound at the hands and feet. The Elders called for silence as one of them stood up and addressed everyone. The celebrations had become an annual tradition, a time for dancing and singing, for great food and for everyone around the world to be celebrating the same thing - successfully surviving Armageddon.

For those that were actually there it's never as much of a celebration than a reminder to stop and reflect. That reflection could not have been more poignant. One of the Elders stood up, took a microphone and started to tell the congregation about how the celebration each year reminds us that we need to be resolved never to return to the wicked world from which our congregation was born from. He then goes on to tell everyone that the three young men bound and gagged and kneeling on the floor before them were found guilty of the sin of homosexuality and for coupling without the consent of the Elders.

I instantly knew where this was leading to. There had been directions from the Society that slowly morphed and changed over the past couple of decades about the need to keep the New World clean and safe from a return to wickedness. This was going to be the latest incarnation of those directions. We all knew the three youngsters. They were all around 20 years old, which in the New World meant they were merely babies. The parents had been kept away from the celebrations, but some of the extended family were present and didn't seem remotely upset or bothered by what was about to happen. In fact the look on their faces were looks of disappointment and disgust at the three young men crying out their hearts and shaking with fear before the row of Elders sat behind them. The Elder with the microphone announced that they are to be a lesson to those that oppose the New World and the laws of God's Society.

With that, the young men were all taken to the stack of wood and tree trunks in the centre of the celebrations amongst whoops, cheers and singing and each one was strapped to a tree trunk. I prayed quietly and inwardly that this was not going the way it looked to be going. I asked God why these young boys would be deserving of death. I didn't even know if they could be killed, after all we lived in a perfect world were we didn't grow sick or age or die, naturally anyway.

I wondered how on earth being homosexual actually harmed anyone. Surely being gay wasn't an influence of the decay or debauchery of the old world as they never knew anything of the old world. They were all of this world, this New World, this perfect world. Surely they were perfect, and as perfect humans how could they be sinning? They would have known the risks as well. They weren't so young and naïve so as to be ignorant. They must have been compelled through nature alone to seek love between themselves and not heterosexually. I didn't understand the world I lived in anymore.

Those next moments were horrific. The bonfire was lit to cheers and laughter. The poor boys burned for an hour before their screams finally halted. Their perfect bodies refused to break down and die. But die they eventually did.

It was a wakeup call to many of those of us that felt lost and confused as to why we were there and where God and the Society were leading us. Those three boys' deaths just added to the guilt of the billions of lives I already felt strongly responsible for.

It was the next day that the final reason to leave this sick, twisted and hellish world was declared to everyone. A special meeting at the Kingdom Hall had been called the day after the celebrations. There was an announcement made by the Elders which had come directly from the headquarters of the Society to every human around the Earth.

Preparations were underway to make the 100th celebration of the end of Armageddon the start of the next chapter in the human race. Every human on the Earth was going to be blessed with total perfect life in the New Order. The last missing component of a perfect human was to be added to return the human race back to the full perfection that Adam and Eve originally enjoyed. The paradise would be ready for that anniversary as all attempts were to be made to finish off the last of the work to clean the Earth for that special date.

In a fanfare of music and applause, it was declared by the Elder on the platform at the Kingdom Hall that on that celebration day in the year 100, the last trait of the old world would be removed from the world of perfect humans.

Free will! It was free will that God was going to remove from all humans around the whole Earth. Free will, they argued, was a disease introduced by the devil, which introduced imperfection, disease and finally death to all human kind. God, they said, was going to restore that imbalance and return man back to his natural state and be like the rest of nature, back in line with God's creations.

That night I met with a few close and dear friends. We all agreed that this announcement was the last that we could bear from this New World. That was not what we had been promised. That was not in alignment with my conscience. This was not good, pure or moral. The human race was about to end and I had been on the wrong side all that time. The guilt hit home for every one of our small group. This was not our dream. It was not our world. It never had been and we felt the filth of a hundred years on our souls.

EVIDENCE 569832D
STATEMENT FROM PC LOUISE GILLARD

24TH FEBRUARY 1976

I was called to the District Hospital to a woman called Anna McPhearson who was awakening from injuries sustained from an assault in her home. I had seen the notes from the Police Officer that had been at the scene so I was familiar with the incident in which she was involved. I knew that it was vital to try and get a statement as quickly as possible from Anna as soon as she awoke before she could be put under any external influence or before she could forget any vital details.

When I got to her bedside she wasn't actually fully awake and aware. Anna kept talking and mumbling and so I made sure that I sat by her bed and took shorthand notes of everything she was saying in case there was anything that could be used as evidence.

The transcript marked 569832C is the whole evening's transcript of what Anna said to me as she drifted in and out of consciousness during the rest of the day and late into the evening. I'm not a psychologist, but it did seem quite obvious that the emotional trauma of both her relationship with her husband Steve McPhearson and the struggle with her Christian conscience was playing out to its furthest reach.

It was very early in the morning of the next day that Anna finally fully regained consciousness. Immediately she wanted to know why she was in a bed covered in bandages. She stated that she was 121 years of age and hadn't suffered ailments for over a hundred years. Anna was confused and clearly upset. She didn't understand why she was in a sick bed at all. I asked her to recall anything from the last time that she saw Steven McPhearson, but she said that she had hardly any recollection of the last time that she saw her husband except for little snippets of memories, and kept repeating that it was difficult to remember details after more than a century had passed by.

I knew that I had to convince her that since the last time she saw her husband, months and not decades had only passed by.

The nurses told me to go back the next morning and give her mind a chance to try and recover from being in a coma for several months. So I took my leave and aimed to return the next day with some aids to help her recall as much as possible.

When I got to Anna's bedside that next morning, Anna looked a lot more aware of her surroundings and interacted a lot better and clearer. Anna admitted that the pain she was feeling was not conducive to the perfect ailment free life she thought she had. I showed her a copy of today's newspaper and pointed out the date was 1976. I could see from her reaction that the truth finally started to be realised which she told me it made her feel dizzy and sick.

I tried to explain to Anna that it was her neighbour that had heard the commotion going off in Anna's house that night and after Steven McPhearson had driven off in his car, the neighbour went around to the house to check if everything was ok. The neighbour found the front door open and called inside but got no answer. The neighbour went in the house and found Anna lying on the carpet, with a severe gash in her head and blood soaking the floor. She called an ambulance straight away and the paramedics managed to save Anna's life.

Anna then starts to recall those last moments, lying on the carpet with her blood running down her head and soaking up unto the carpet. She recalls her husband sitting there in front of her as she started to fade and slip away. Then she remembers Steve getting up and walking out into the night and hearing the car start up and power away down the street. Anna started to cry as she recalled the feeling of abandonment and loneliness and remembers praying to God and asking his forgiveness.

Anna asks where her family and friends are. One of the nurses goes through with Anna how at first family and people from the congregation came every day to see her; some even sat by her bedside and read to her. But as the weeks passed the visits got fewer and fewer, and as the months passed only one person regularly came to see her anymore and her name was Mary.

It was by some miracle of coincidence that her friend Mary from church then arrived at that very moment after she had got word that Anna was out of her coma and awake. Anna and Mary embraced as friends.

I kept to one side and listened to Mary finally convince Anna that it was only 1976 and that she had been in the bed where she now lies for what had been several months. Anna then explained to Mary where she thought she had been, how she lived this other life and the repercussions of it. It took Anna a couple of hours to tell Mary all the details of this other life that Anna had lived while Mary sat and patiently listened. It was at the end of her story and explaining the shock of being back in 1976 that Anna's face changed, as though a thought had suddenly changed her entire demeanour. Anna told Mary how she was willing to give it all up, how she was willing to sacrifice her life to not be a part of the Jehovah's Witnesses anymore, that God's plan was not something that her conscience could live with and went on to explain the sheer relief of having a second chance and being back in the present with a whole new life ahead of her.

Mary broke her silence and asked Anna if she really understood the consequences of her what she was saying. By denouncing God, Anna would turn her back on the whole congregation and also the whole of her family. Anna would be alone, cut off from everyone she knew and all her friends would not be allowed to even talk to her. Mary pleaded with Anna to reconsider, because they would not be friends anymore if she carried through with what Anna was deciding to do. But instead of changing her mind, Anna actually tried to persuade Mary that actually, Mary was on the wrong side. Anna pleaded with Mary to not make the same mistake she had made for a hundred years, begged her not to side with genocide, bigotry and cruelty. The fact that her closest friend was willing to turn her back and shun her, Anna pleaded, surely went against every thread of good conscience. But Mary was adamant that if Anna kept on insisting, with immediate effect, Mary would have to leave. Anna did keep on trying to reason with Mary that Mary was responsible for the actions of the organisation she is a part of, that ignorance is not a valid excuse for ignoring the cruelty to your fellow man and the primary rule to love everyone should be the only law anyone needs.

Both of them could tell that neither would persuade the other that they were right. It was moving to watch them both say their last goodbyes to each other and hold each other while in floods of tears until Mary finally stood up and said goodbye for the last time and left the room.

I didn't resume chatting to Anna for a couple of hours in order to let her settle. I vowed to Anna that although she was a case of Domestic Violence and that the Police typically see those cases as a "private affair between a husband and wife", the seriousness of the assault in my opinion merited a charge of attempted murder. I'm already being warned to drop the case and to not get personally involved by not just my fellow Police Officers but also my superiors. My only concern is the mental state of the victim Anna and whether or not she can be used reliably enough in any public trial.

I feel I have a duty to Anna. What I witnessed today was one of the bravest breaks of independence I have ever witnessed from a person. Not only is she breaking free from a violent husband, she has just broke free from a tightly controlling and all-consuming religious way of life, not because it's an easy option, but because her principles and moral set will not allow her with good conscience to carry on with a belief system she know is wrong for her.

It was only later that evening that Anna really got me to understand how much she had given up. She had not just decided to not go to church anymore, she had decided that the faith she had and the belief system she had was wrong and if asked, Anna felt the need to be truthful and honest and say that the beliefs of the Jehovah's Witnesses was akin to fascism and she couldn't align herself with that anymore. This would be seen by The Society as apostasy and as such would be punished by the Society that she wanted nothing more to do with. That meant excommunication, or disfellowshipping as the Jehovah's Witnesses call it.

Unfortunately, because her own family, all her friends, in fact everyone she knew was in that faith, that meant that no-one she currently knew would ever speak to her again. All ties, conversations and social connections have to be cut from a person when they are disfellowshipped, even if they are your close family.

Anna, after a life of over a hundred years, was now totally alone.

UK NATIONAL NEWSPAPER
FULL PAGE ARTICLE ON PAGE 7

14TH MARCH 2017

It has been forty years since the nation was fascinated by the trial of Steven McPhearson, who was accused of attempted murder in 1977. The trial became a landmark in British justice and although Steven McPhearson was found not guilty, the perception of domestic violence by the Police was also put on trial by the public and by the media.

The trial revolved around Anna McPhearson, now remarried as Anna Bailey. Anna was the former wife of Steven McPhearson. They lived a modest and devoutly religious life in the north of England. Anna was found close to death by a neighbour who had heard the married couple arguing and then saw Steven McPhearson drive away in his car at a fast speed. The neighbour found the McPhearson's front door open and so went into the house to find Anna bleeding to death from a head wound lying on the living room floor.

The ambulance service managed to save Anna's life, but

Anna spent several months in a coma in hospital. It was only once Anna awoke from the coma that Police Constable Louise Gillard was able to interview Anna and enough evidence could be collected to prosecute Steven McPhearson.

The trial itself divided the nation. Many said the trial was a waste of the taxpayers money and it exposed severe gender bias in the Police Force as Police Constable Louise Gillard leaked evidence to the press that several high ranking Police Officers and Super Intendants, warned Police Constable Louise Gillard that domestic violence was not the business of the Police Force. In early 1977 when the trial was half way through proceedings, a huge rally was staged in the centre of London to protest against the ingrained gender biased in all our government institutions.

There was a period of roughly six months in the beginning of 1977 where all political and social discussion in the UK was about nothing else but the bias deeply rooted in our society against equality for women. The Steven McPhearson trial was at the centre of all those discussions.

Steven McPhearson was eventually cleared of all charges. His defence attacked Anna McPhearson's mental state and accused Anna that her memories were distorted recollections used to bolster the verbal evidence from Anna's testimony. There were many accusations after the trial that even extreme bias in the jury and the courts skewed the verdict and that a fair trial was never actually possible. A public enquiry resulted and in the three years the enquiry ran for found massive gender bias in all government departments and made recommendations that are still being implemented and felt today.

Anna Bailey now lives with her new husband in the north of England and has two children who are now both parents themselves. But she also has had to endure a long period of isolation and loneliness on top of the anxieties of the trial and the publicity that it exposed Anna to. When married to Steven McPhearson, both Anna and Stephen were practicing Jehovah's Witnesses. The name of this Christian doomsday religion may be familiar to many as the people that knock on your door and preach the beliefs of the religion and sell their magazine The Watchtower. But since the trial ended, Stephen and Anna divorced. Steven was disfellowshipped from the religion, which is a form of excommunication and expulsion from the church.

Anna's experience of abuse and the way it was handled by the church helped her come to the decision to also leave the religion also. "My conscience wouldn't allow me to be part of a faith that has at its core belief, genocide, sexism and homophobia" says Anna of her decision to leave the church. But that decision has had far reaching repercussions for Anna as a person openly denying being part of Jehovah's Witnesses, she has also been shunned from her whole extended family and every friend she used to know.

"When I came out of the hospital, I didn't know anyone in the world, as my family and all the friends I had in the world, turned their back on me, shunned me and refused to even talk to me. It was a very difficult time. It was another year until I met my husband to be".

Stephen McPhearson himself remarried, but then divorced for a second time ten years later.

Anna plays down her role in bringing domestic violence into the public consciousness, "I don't want to be known as a victim" she said when asked about her role in history. "I taught my children that violence against anyone is a sin against humanity. I have also brought them up to believe that all genders are equal and standing up for equality is the legacy I would like to be remembered for".

Former Superintendent Louise Gillard stated;
"Anna Bailey should be celebrated as a national hero. Anna was not only brave enough to stand against her husband, but also face up with dignity against a hostile, gender biased prosecution. How do you face people that think you deserve to be violently abused because that is seen as your role in life? Then she was faced with an impossible decision to choose between her family and friends or choose the side of her conscience. Despite all that she has lost, Anna Bailey stuck to her conscience and moral sense of right and wrong. That is real strength. She is the strongest woman I have ever met and I am proud to have once been able to stand beside her."

There is a growing movement online to provide support for all those suffering at the hand of this horrendous cult. Since leaving the Jehovah's Witnesses religion nearly thirty years ago, I have never known there to be so much love and care available for anyone that finds themselves questioning "the Truth".

You are not alone, just reach out.

www.Xjwfriends.com
Website, twitter, facebook and Instagram

www.jonnyhalfhead.com
Also available on Amazon by this author - Nine Pills

ABOUT THE AUTHOR

Jonny Halfhead grew up as a third generation Jehovah's Witness. As one of Jehovah's Witnesses for twenty years, he experienced a thorough immersion in its doctrines and practices. Although never baptised, he was raised under a very strict regime that always made him different and stand out from everyone else around him, even others in the same faith.

When circumstances ejected him from that controlling and all-encompassing lifestyle, he was in a unique position to follow his love of music and expand his imagination as an all-round artist. Jonny Halfhead started a Gothic music fanzine in the early nineties in an attempt to find musicians and join a band. The band he joined was called 13 Candles, which he joined as a keyboard player and grew as a singer until he split to form his own band called Personality Crisis in 1994.

Failure to keep a live band together meant turning Personality Crisis into a studio only band for the next decade and more.

In 2012 Jonny Halfhead started an online blog about his hobby of collecting the music of the famous independent music label 4AD with the aim on exhibiting his collection on the labels 50th anniversary in 2030. After a few years the blog entries started to dwindle as it became more difficult to collect and stick to the high expectations and costs placed he placed upon his own collection promise.

In 2018 Jonny Halfhead released his first short story "Nine Pills" through Amazon, which had many elements based on his youth as being one of Jehovah's Witnesses and the struggles involved with being associated with a cult.

Printed in Great Britain
by Amazon

10828902R00078